THOMAS

By

Michael G. Manning

FT
Pbk

Cover by Amalia Chitulescu
Editing by Grace Bryan Butler
ISBN: 978-1-943481-08-8

For more information about the Mageborn series check
out the author's Facebook page:

https://www.facebook.com/MagebornAuthor

or visit the website:

http://www.magebornbooks.com/

CHAPTER 1
SARAH

Shrouded in the mists of his childhood, Thomas' earliest memories were of the cold. The cold, and a near endless hunger; the sort that made him feel as though his innards were devouring him from within. He could hardly remember being warm, much less full. He was alone, a street waif, without parent or guardian, and no recollection of ever having been anything but...

The day he came across a kitten, wet and mewing in an alley, was different. It would be the first day he remembered well, for it was the first day that anything important happened to him. Lost and hungry, the kitten seemed much like himself, and despite the fact that he had nothing to offer, he felt drawn to it. Moving quietly toward the small cat, he made soft reassuring noises, until at last he was able to pick it up.

The poor thing was shivering, much as he was, so he held it close against him, to share what little warmth his thin cold frame had to offer. Consequently, he didn't notice the figure approaching him. Another person having seen him there, a small boy clutching a wet kitten, would have been moved by the tragedy of it. The person who did find him however, was not prone to such frail emotions.

The young man watching him approached slowly, to avoid alerting his target. His name was Flin, and he was a bully of the worst sort; older, stronger; the son of a merchant, and one look revealed that he hadn't missed any meals. Yet for some reason he was filled with anger, and his free time was generally occupied with finding ways to torment street urchins, or anyone weaker and less fortunate. Maybe he did it from boredom, though not even he knew what drove him to his actions.

Thomas had avoided him many times in the past, nimbly escaping him whenever he came around, but those were better days, when he wasn't so cold, so hungry, and burdened with a kitten. A short run was all he managed before Flin got a solid grip on his arm and spun him about. The kitten went tumbling away, dropping from Thomas' numbed hands. "Wait Flin, don't hurt it!" he cried without thinking.

"You worried about this bit of rags? I figured you'd be more worried about what I'm gonna do to you," said his tormentor. A wicked grin lit the youth's face, showing a cracked tooth. "That's ok; I'll put him out of his misery for ya." Raising his booted foot, he made ready to crush the small animal.

"No!" without thinking Thomas dove down, and shoved the kitten aside. Flin's boot came down hard upon his arm instead, and having trapped it there, Flin began to slowly bear down. "Stop, wait...," Thomas' words faltered. Pain shot up his arm, with a pop and a sickening grinding sensation, he felt the bones in his wrist snap, almost causing him to lose consciousness. A moment later, vision blurred by tears, he saw Flin kneeling, leaning in toward him. A flash caught his attention, the glint from a knife. Returning to his senses, he realized Flin was cutting off his shirt and coat.

"I thought about beating the crap out of a little piss pants like you, but then I figured it would just get my clothes dirty, so maybe I'll just get rid of this shirt for you and see how long it takes you to freeze to death out here..." He stopped talking for a moment, staring at the odd design on Thomas' chest. "What the hell? I knew you was a dirty little bastard, but looks like you're deformed as well as smelly. What is that, a curse mark?" Flin paused for a moment, obviously deep in thought. "Yep it would definitely be a public service to go ahead and put an end to a malformed little shit like you."

The look in his eye as he brought the knife up again left no doubt in Thomas' mind, this was it, the end. It all seemed so useless, but for a moment his first thought was that at least he wouldn't be hungry anymore. Time slowed down a bit, and a small movement caught his eye, the kitten scurrying off. *At least the cat got away,* he thought to himself, and then he heard her voice.

"It's not a birthmark." Her voice was smooth, without a quaver or any sign of fear. She was obviously young, dressed in rags; she looked just a few years older than Thomas. Her face was smooth, but smudged with dirt, not that anyone would notice after seeing her hair, shining red gold, it wreathed her face, spilling out recklessly in all directions. It was everywhere, sticking up from her head, out to the sides, and falling well past her shoulders.

Flin became still for a moment, and then he straightened up and turned to the girl, unsure of himself for some reason.

"It's not a birthmark," she repeated clearly, "but a burn, and not just on his body, but upon his very soul. A curse? Perhaps—but rather a curse of destiny, marking him for my service. Count yourself lucky you were not chosen, although I would not take one as weak of mind and body as you." There was a glint of what might be pure madness in her eyes, which now that he noticed them, were the clearest blue Thomas had ever seen.

"You know what? I don't have time for this." Flin stood up and began to walk carefully away. "Little piss pants, I'm gonna leave you to this crazy bitch." Spitting on the ground, he took his eyes away from her and walked briskly away, something akin to fear showing in the set of his shoulders. Thomas couldn't imagine what would make him act that way, although the newcomer was certainly bold.

Thomas looked back at the girl, wondering for a moment how her hair managed to be so many places at once; then he tried to get up. Forgetting his arm, he tried to lift himself with it, and the pain, forgotten for a moment, came howling back at him, ushering him into cold darkness as he passed out.

When he awoke later, after what seemed days, he found himself in a strange place. Lying on a pile of cotton rags and old burlap sacks, he was warm. Looking over, Thomas realized there was a small fire, illuminating what appeared to be an odd collection of old wooden fruit crates. Sitting up, he felt much better than he had in days, warm at least; that was when his stomach began to loudly remind him he hadn't eaten for some time.

"I figured you'd be hungry, here." There she was, sitting close by, holding a loaf of fresh bread. Without thinking Thomas took it and began to devour it. His stomach hurt at the first bite, having been empty for so long, but he couldn't stop, at least not until he had eaten three quarters of the loaf. Finally, he got control of himself, remembering his beggarly manners.

"Thank you, I'm sorry I ate more than my share. Here, you take the rest." Shy for a reason he couldn't name, he looked at the older girl from under his matted hair, offering her the remainder of the loaf.

Her laughter came to his ears like small silver bells, tinkling without cause or care. She laughed unabashedly at him, but then her face became serious. "I'm not hungry, that was all for you, but I won't dishonor your gift." Taking the loaf from him, she took one small bite. He saw a pearly flash of teeth as she nipped the loaf delicately, then she handed it back, "There, you eat the rest. You need it."

Further encouragement was unnecessary, he quickly ate the remainder; staring at her from the corner of his eye, wondering at her generosity. It was about this time that he realized he was resting his weight on his broken arm, and indeed, had been using it since he awoke. "My wrist! What?"

"Oh, it was fine. I looked you over after you passed out, didn't seem to be more than a mild bruise," she answered in a matter-of-fact manner.

"But it was broken! How? How long have I been asleep? Did you do something to my arm?" his confusion spilled out, but her look stilled his questions.

"No, it's fine, but if you like we can break it now. Would that be better?" her face was lit with a mischievous smile. He would learn with time that she had a rather odd sense of humor, for that was the beginning of the best year of his life. Her name was Sarah, and she lived in a back alley between the docks and the trade district.

Her collection of fruit crates came to seem like a castle to him, a place of security. She wouldn't let him live there, valuing her own privacy, but whenever it was too cold, or he was in need, she would let him stay for a day or two here and there. The rest of the time he was allowed to visit, often for hours at a stretch, although the price seemed to be participation in her odd games, or listening to her fanciful stories. Not that he minded, for the first time in his short life, he got to be a child, rather than just a street orphan.

Thomas was about ten years of age at this time, but she appeared a bit older, probably around thirteen, not that she ever told him. The games she liked seemed more suited to children younger than both of them, but he played them gladly anyway.

"Are you ready Thomas?" she said loudly one day, using her high court voice, an essential part of their latest game.

"Yes, milady," he replied, trying his best to imitate a nobleman's cultured tones.

"No, no, no, it's not 'milady' until *after* you've sworn the oath!"

"Oh, right. Yes, Your Majesty!"

"Your Grace will do, I am not a queen after all," her act was marred by a slight smirk as she said this.

"Yes, Your Grace," he answered soberly.

"Do you swear to serve me all your life, with all your strength, all your mind, body and soul? To protect the..."

"I swear on my life," he interrupted, having thought she was done.

"Let me finish!" Sighing, she continued, "To protect the weak, show mercy to the helpless, giving aid to the downtrodden, and undertaking any task I might give to you."

"I so swear."

"On your soul," she corrected.

"Why on my soul? I said on my life earlier, what's the difference?" Sometimes her games had odd rules.

"Because I am taking your service, not just in this life, but in the life hereafter, and any to come from thence forward," she answered imperiously.

"That doesn't make much sense; I mean I don't even know what's going to happen when I die and nobody really..."

"Are you going to swear or not?" for a moment her eyes blazed and Thomas felt unsure, an unusual thing, since normally he never felt more at ease than when he was playing with Sarah.

That's right, this is Sarah. The thought came to him with a sudden realization, even if it weren't a game, he had never cared about anyone more. A resolve built within him, and he answered her in his normal voice, without a hint of mockery. "I swear, all the above, on my soul, for this life and the next, and any to come after that, I will never forsake you, nor forget my duty." Looking up into her eyes, the sun flared behind her, illuminating her hair like a fiery wreath. He saw a triumphant look on her face as she gazed down upon him. *She may not be a queen, but she certainly looks like one to me.*

"It is right that those who offer to us unbroken fidelity should be protected by our aid. And since you, a faithful one of ours, have seen fit to swear trust and fidelity to us in our hand, therefore we decree and command that you shall ever be sheltered by us and given succor in time of need."

"Where did you learn that?" Thomas questioned.

"Wot? Did ya think I din't know me letters?" she answered in a playful accent.

"You're impossible!" he blustered, turning red as the moment passed.

"Just remember, Tommy, you're still just a small boy, therefore I only expect you to care for kittens and small animals at this point. But I will expect much more of you in the future!" she told him, her tone serious once more.

He could never really tell when she was serious or when she was joking around, but he figured he could manage kittens.

CHAPTER 2
WHITMIRE

A year passed, as the happy days of youth often do, so quickly that Thomas hardly noticed it. This was the first good year Thomas could remember, so it caught him quite by surprise when winter began nearing again. The day was cold, as winter was returning with a vengeance. As so often happened, Thomas sought Sarah in what he thought of as her castle. Her haven among the fruit crates.

As usual, she had managed to find plenty of food. It was fresh fruit today. He often wondered how she got so much, but she never revealed her secrets. Looking at her now, he studied her smudged face. There was something almost ethereal about Sarah, her face was vaguely dirty but her skin always had a glow about it. Her hair, wild and unkempt, still managed to shine brilliantly, even though he couldn't imagine how she would have managed to wash it. For that matter, she always smelled good too.

Today she looked sad.

"I figured you'd show up today," she said, "but you can't stay."

"That's ok, but it is really cold out." Thomas was rather disappointed, for a moment caught up wondering where he'd find a warm enough spot for the night. It wasn't the first time she had turned him away, but never when the weather was cruel as it was now. Secretly he had always suspected she turned him away merely to keep him self-reliant.

"I have to go Thomas." The words brought him back to the present and something in her tone worried him.

"Where are you going?"

"I can't stay a girl forever. I have things I have to do."

"Well of course we're growing up, but you don't have to act so serious about it," even as he said it, Thomas knew he was misunderstanding her. "If you just tell me what's going on, maybe I can help."

Sarah smiled, "You'll help more than you realize, but that's for another day."

"But..."

"Don't worry; I've planned ahead for you." Sometimes she seemed to really believe she was some sort of feudal liege. It was endearing and yet still made him wonder if she was a few cards shy of a full deck. But he put his doubts aside, since he could tell she was serious, and for some reason it sparked an angry feeling within him.

"What do you mean?" he asked.

"I have a friend. A man named Whitmire. He'll be at the Crown Tavern tonight. He'll give you a place to stay," her voice had a sadness to it.

"Is that where you've been getting your food!?" Thomas was angry, but uncertain. He'd often wondered how she found food so often, now her statements made him rethink everything.

"Of course not! Now shut up and listen to me. This is important, Thomas. You need to remember what I tell you. Remember it well," her voice had taken on that tone she used when they were playing their high court games. Yet something about it made him stop.

"Go in, you'll find him at the bar. Tell him that you're a friend of mine. He may not believe you at first, but if you show him your birthmark, he will know what to do."

"You expect me to go into a *bar*, and tell a complete stranger that a crazy girl named Sarah sent me, and then pull off my shirt and show him my birthmark? And then he's gonna suddenly decide to take me in? Have you gone crazy?" Thomas couldn't hide his derision now, but behind it was a deeper desperation. He could tell he was losing the only person who had ever cared about him.

"Yes, tell him that you know me. Show him your mark, and he'll understand. And one other thing..." she added.

"Yes, milady?" His voice was wooden, and he used a formal tone normally reserved for their games, but in this case, he knew she would feel his anger and pain. This was no game.

"Tell him that even if he has forgotten me, I have not forgotten him."

"What the hell does that mean?" He was near shouting now. Standing up, he could feel his face turning red. But then she was there—wrapping her arms around him. The smell of cedar and sandalwood enveloped him, carried by her wild hair. He could feel her tears on his shoulder. For a moment, he forgot everything until her voice continued.

"Don't forget, Thomas. Remember this year."

She wouldn't listen after that, wouldn't argue, wouldn't discuss. She calmly sent him on his way. Her attitude was firm and before he knew it, Thomas was walking down the cold alleyway, hardly daring to look back.

He would always remember that day sadly, for it was the last time he saw her. In the days and months that followed, he would return on occasion, looking for her, but her castle was gone. In its place, he found only a moldering rubbish pile. No sign of her remained, and no one recalled the wild strawberry blonde who held court in alleyways and sent her servant on errands to rescue birds and kittens.

That night he found his way to the Crown Tavern. The cold was biting, so he didn't pause long before entering, despite the fact that he'd never entered a tavern before. Inside a roaring blaze kept the patrons warm, and the air held a collection of smells, from spilt beer to old straw, to the smell of people themselves. It felt good to him, yet he knew from past experiences in shops, once the adults noticed him, he'd be back out on the street in short order. No one wanted a ratty vagrant child around.

He'd already made a plan to find Whitmire, one that would hopefully get him to Whitmire quickly and avoid the problem of being tossed out before he could find him. Taking a deep breath, he strode up to the bar, "Excuse me sir." He addressed the bartender. "I've been sent with a message for a Mister Whitmire, is he here tonight?"

The barkeep's eyes swept him from head to toe, his visage displaying clearly what he thought of beggars in his establishment. He stared for a moment, his hesitation making Thomas wonder if his idea was as clever as he had at first thought. "*Father* Whitmire is over there in the corner, but he's nigh well pickled this evening, so I doubt he'll hear you. Mind you though, if I catch you rifling pockets in here, I'll have your ears off!" He pointed to the far corner, where a man slumped in a wooden chair.

Thomas thanked the man and moved toward the corner. Behind him the barkeep spoke again, "Remember I'm watching you boy!"

As if I could forget. Thomas thought to himself. He was again filled with doubt, but glancing down, he saw his sword, and it brought back his resolve. Although he thought of it as his 'sword', it was merely a thin branch he used for that purpose when playing with Sarah. He wasn't sure why he had brought it, stuffed clumsily through a bit of cord tied around his waist, but it made him feel better anyway.

Stepping up to the table, he saw that the man named Whitmire seemed asleep. His clothing was well made, though not rich or ostentatious in its cut or material. He wore no armor, but a scimitar hung at his waist. As he got closer Thomas could smell the alcohol, a dangerous scent to a boy on the street, for drunks were wont to show little restraint. "Excuse me sir."

Whitmire's left eye eased open slowly. "What?" he mumbled.

"A friend of mine, a girl named Sarah asked me to bring you a message and to ask a favor." Thomas managed to get all the main points into one sentence, hoping to get the man's attention.

Whitmire waved his arm vaguely in Thomas' direction, "Go away, I've nothing to give, and I've nothing to do with any girls, named Sarah or otherwise." His voice was thick and slurred, but his accent was clear enough that Thomas could still understand them. He could also sense a dangerous undercurrent of apathy and anger.

Inwardly, he was confused, *Why in the hell would she send me to find some drunk? Does she really know this man?* "She said you might not believe me at first, but that I should show you this..." He began pulling up his shirt, certain that he was about to be thrown out. *This has to be the most embarrassing thing she's ever asked me to do.*

Before he could get his shirt up the man recoiled, "By the light! Are you addled boy! I may be a drunk, but I've never been *that* sort of priest! Get the hell away from me!" Roaring, Whitmire was standing now, staring down at Thomas, his face flushed with alcohol and rage. For a moment, Thomas feared he would strike him, but the moment passed, as Whitmire looked about the room, full now of staring eyes, watching the display. "I'm leaving, barkeep. I'll pay my due tomorrow, you know I'm good for it!" Pushing Thomas back, he nearly stumbled over a chair, and made his way to the door.

Stunned, Thomas sat down, his mind blank until a large fist gripped his shirt collar and jerked him up. "I warned you boy, you shouldn't think you can come in here and mess with *my* customers!" With a rough toss the barkeep put Thomas across the nearest table. A second later, Thomas felt a searing pain as the barkeep brought a leather belt to bear on the struggling boy. At first Thomas twisted and turned, seeking a quick escape, but after a moment he surrendered. Past experiences with angry shopkeepers had taught him that struggling merely prolonged a beating.

After what seemed like an eternity, the barman's arm finally got tired. Still muttering curses under his breath, he let go of Thomas, who promptly jumped and ran for the door, blinking back tears. The strapping felt as though it had set his back afire, from his shoulders to his knees. Without thought he tumbled into the street, before picking himself up and running toward the nearest alley. Humiliation had been his near constant companion for years, the years before he met Sarah, so it felt almost normal to him as he ran for cover, but what he found in the alley was anything but normal.

There, in the dim light, he could see a man stretched out on the cold stone, while another man searched hastily through his pockets. No stranger to the streets, Thomas knew immediately what he was seeing. A heavy truncheon was held steady in the grip of a third man. *That's the lookout,* Thomas realized instantly. The man with the heavy wooden weapon had already seen him and nudged his companion as he prepared to deal with the intrusion.

Thomas knew that chances were good, if he just turned and ran, that they wouldn't bother following him. Most likely they'd finish their theft and be off as quickly as possible, but Thomas had just been strapped. His only friend was gone, and his only hope had rejected him. He was empty, and consequently his instinct for survival had apparently abandoned him. Within the emptiness, he felt a sudden flame in his heart that was neither rage, nor a suicidal impulse. *This has got to stop!* Fear was replaced by the memory of Sarah that day when she stopped Flin.

"Get away from him." The voice shocked him with its calm, even more when he realized it was his own voice rising from some deep recess within. Reaching down, he drew his stick. He knew it was a hopeless gesture, but he did it just the same. Recalling his pledge to Sarah, he raised it menacingly, an almost comical gesture for a ten year old boy facing two grown men.

The man with the truncheon laughed. "What do you plan to do with that twig boy? This ain't a game. You best run home, or you'll get worse than this drunken priest!"

The fire inside him bloomed incandescent, and he heard a voice, his own, answering, "I have sworn, to my lady Sarah, to defend the weak and protect the helpless." With that he raised his stick, as if to strike, when something astonishing happened. Light blossomed in the dark alley, radiating from the golden flames that now wreathed his flimsy weapon, enfolding the wood without burning it.

The thugs' faces were lit in stark contrast by the blazing light, shock clearly written in their features. Slowly, they backed away, step by step and finally turned and ran, not speaking a word. Looking down, Thomas eventually realized that the man on the ground was awake and staring at him. "Are you ok, mister?"

That was when he recognized the man as Whitmire. He looked the worse for his time on the cobblestones, but his gaze no longer seemed as unsteady. A trickle of blood ran down the back of his neck as he sat up. "Sarah didn't tell me you were a priest, or I wouldn't have bothered you before..." Thomas' words trailed off while at the same time the flames on his stick slowly flickered out, reminding him that something well beyond his understanding had just occurred.

"Truthfully, I'm a disgrace of a priest if I must be honest. I've barely done more than drink these past couple of years," answered Whitmire.

Thomas ignored his confession, more interested in the recent display of magic, "How did you make my sword burst into flames like that?! That was the most amazing thing I've ever seen, like something out of the stories!"

"Your sword?" Father Whitmire suppressed a chuckle, along with a wave of nausea. "I didn't do that—I'd guess your goddess did, as much a reminder to me as to those thugs, of her power, and mercy." He slowly stood, and then looked at Thomas. He was uncomfortably sober now, although waves of dizziness threatened to send his stomach contents tumbling out. "I'm sorry about before, I didn't realize you were a follower, nor one so honored as to receive the Lady's direct intervention. I think I may have done a great disservice to you, young man."

"I don't have a goddess, I serve my lady Sarah." The words felt childish to Thomas even as the memory brought tears to his eyes.

"You mentioned her before, but I'm afraid I still don't know who you're talking about. I can tell you that what you saw tonight is one of the most famous signs shown by my goddess, Delwyn. When one of her disciples is in danger, she sometimes blesses their weapons with her divine fire. Although, it is highly uncommon for her to show such favor except during the Festival of the Sun, many months from now. You must be someone special for her to show favor at a time like this, especially at night."

"Maybe it was because I was trying to help you," Thomas was growing more confused as the conversation went on, not the least because he'd almost never had an adult showing any measure of respect toward him.

"I doubt it, I've not been the best of servants these past few years," said the priest. Suddenly, Father Whitmire doubled over, and began to wretch into the gutter. After several minutes, he finally stood back up, though still unsteady. "Well, the least I can do is get you a meal after all that, and listen to your request and whatever message you have for me."

Thomas' stomach began to grumble at the thought of food, even though he'd had some fruit just half a day gone. "Sarah told me to ask you for a place to stay, and her message was very short."

"Given the circumstances, I'm sure I could shelter you for a week or two, no more. The temple cannot afford to take in everyone that needs food and shelter."

"She also told me to show you this," red-faced, Thomas once again pulled up his shirt, showing the older man his bizarre birthmark.

In the dark alley, it was hard to tell, but it looked as though Father Whitmire had gone very pale. "What message did she ask you to give me?" his voice low, not quite a whisper.

"It wasn't much of a message. Honestly, she's a little crazy if you ask me, but she said to tell you that even if you had forgotten her, she had not forgotten you."

CHAPTER 3
GROM

It had been a year since that night in the alley with Father Whitmire. Thomas was now living at the temple in a small cell. The priest had changed his mind about letting him stay, but hadn't fully explained his reasons. Apparently, something that night had affected him though, for Father Whitmire had stopped going to bars and avoided strong drink completely now.

Life, as a whole, was both easier and more complicated than it had been before. Thomas was no longer hungry, or even cold. The temple provided simple food, but it was always hot. His bed was barely more than a hard, wooden frame with worn down cotton batting padding it, but combined with an old wool blanket and a nearly flat pillow, it was the most comfortable thing he had ever slept on.

His days were fairly busy; he was attending the temple school with other boys. Their ages varied, and probably all told, there were only about twenty or so of them at any given time. The temple had two schools, one for boys and one for girls, although there weren't many of them. In each case the classes were so small that all the ages were in one classroom.

Thomas was a bit of an oddity at the school, since all the other children came from families with money; a sizable donation was usually given to the temple in return for their education. None of them were from higher nobility of course, those fortunates had private tutors. Most of the boys were third sons, being trained in preparation for someday joining the clergy, a few were young second sons, preparing for a military career. The only firstborns were sons of merchants, there to learn numbers and letters so they could someday help their fathers' businesses.

In any case, they were all better than him, and they knew it. Most were fairly nice, especially the younger boys. But a couple of them liked to make sure he knew exactly where he stood, as a charity case, admitted purely upon the generosity of the temple. Thomas didn't let it bother him much, after years of privation and cold, the attitudes of a few didn't seem quite so important to him, and he'd always been pretty level-headed.

He took to numbers and letters rather quickly, his young mind absorbing knowledge like a dry sponge. Although he started out far behind the others, within a year he was doing better than many of the second and third year students at arithmetic and reading. Thanks to his success in class he'd even had some luck making friends with some of the younger students.

During lunches he often sat with his new friend, Sam. Sam was an earnest boy, if not terribly bright, but he always made the conversations at the table livelier. Today however, he was a bit more muted, probably because Ivan was sitting on the other side of him. Ivan was the third son of a minor baron, and as such seemed to think he was much better than most of the other boys, even though he was probably destined to become a member of the clergy, much like them. Thomas was wondering how long they'd have to put up with him when Grom came in and sat down with his tray at the end of the table.

Grom was unusual to say the least; he was short and broad with a thick full beard. That would've been remarkable in and of itself, except for the fact that he was a dwarf. Thomas supposed that most dwarves must look like that, although he had no experience to know for sure. The dwarf had been at the temple for a couple of years before Thomas was taken in, but he'd rarely seen him at the table. Grom ate at a different time most days, probably to avoid drawing so much attention as he did now.

"They shouldn't let dogs eat at the table—they might get the impression they're people," Ivan said this in a soft tone, loud enough that the boys could hear him but softly enough that he wouldn't earn Brother Simon's reproach. The stern priest sat at the other end of the table.

This finally brought Sam out of his self-imposed silence, "You shouldn't say things like that."

"Didn't you hear why he's here?" Ivan spoke in a conspiratorial whisper. "He lured a shopkeeper's son to his smithy, and killed him."

"That's crazy talk," Thomas cut in, "They wouldn't let him live here at the temple if he'd done something like that." Ivan's air of importance annoyed him.

"No, it's true! They couldn't prove it because they never found the body. Father Whitmire was at the court hearing. Supposedly, he talked 'em into paroling him to the temple. Just like him, Whitmire will bring any mangy old dog into the temple." This last remark was indirectly pointed at Thomas. One of Ivan's favorite barbs was to liken him to a stray since as an orphan he had no sponsor. "He probably cooked the kid and ate him. Everyone knows dwarves will eat anything."

Thomas stood up, he'd listened to enough, and he knew Ivan was trying to bait him into an argument. "I better get going. I don't want to be late." He had plenty of time, but he figured heading to kitchen duty was better than listening to Ivan's rant.

"Better watch out Tommy, you know that dwarf sleeps just a few cells down on your floor. I bet he'd love another stray dog for dinner." Ivan's face was lit with a malicious grin, but Thomas ignored it and headed off for the kitchen. He was surprised to hear that Grom's room was so near his own, in two years he'd never seen him leaving or entering, although he had passed him in the hallway once or twice.

Later that evening Thomas sat in the courtyard. It was a pleasant day and he really didn't have much to do after completing his chores. Some days he would go back to his room and read, but the weather was so nice that it seemed a waste. Consequently, he was watching the birds, and thinking about Sarah. Sunny days often reminded him of her.

Presently, he noticed the sound of a hammer, ringing away in the temple smithy. He'd heard it before, but today's lunch conversation had made him curious. Rising from his seat, he wandered in the direction of the forge building. It was an open-air construction, to provide good ventilation, and positioned well away from the rest of the temple buildings, probably to avoid disturbing the priests, the noise from it was pretty loud after all.

Drawing closer, he saw the dwarf engrossed in his labor. He was working away at an iron bar, beating upon it with an oddly shaped hammer. The striking end of the hammer was rounded, and with each strike the bar flattened and stretched out. *I suppose that's fullering.* Thomas thought, remembering a brief lesson on metal work from the year before. Grom's back was turned to him, and he seemed fully absorbed by his work. Thomas stood quietly, not wanting to interrupt, not certain if he should be there at all.

After a time, the hammer stopped. "If you're not too busy gawking, grab those gloves and work the bellows," Grom spoke without turning around. As he lifted the bar and returned it to the forge to reheat, his arms stood out with corded muscle. Surprised, Thomas was still for a moment, and then quickly moved to do as the dwarf had asked.

Several hours later, Thomas was exhausted. The heat from the forge had left him drenched in sweat, while his arms ached from pumping the bellows. Grom seemed unfazed. *Maybe dwarves really are made of stone,* but Thomas quickly dismissed the thought.

"You'd better get cleaned up, lest your bed wind up smelling like burnt iron." Grom's voice was deep and gravelly, but not unkind. The nine o'clock bells rang in the distance.

"Oh!" Thomas realized he was almost too late, if he didn't clean up quickly, he'd be late for lights out in the dormitory. That would surely make Brother Simon angry. "Thanks for letting me watch!" He darted out of the smithy, the late hour giving him the energy he needed to run back to the dorm.

Grom shook his head as he watched the boy run off. *Guess that'll teach him to hang around,* he thought. *Still, he did stick around for a while.*

The next few days passed uneventfully, and Thomas had plenty of sore muscles from his experience at the forge. Still his time with the taciturn dwarf had only made him more curious. *He didn't seem like a murderer.* Although he had to admit, he had no clue what a homicidal dwarf would be like. Either way, he was fairly sure Grom wasn't evil, much less an eater of children.

Toward the end of the week, he went back to the smithy. This time he began working the bellows as soon as Grom set something in the forge to heat.

"Grab that apron if you're gonna stick around again. Don't want you ruining your clothes." The dwarf waved at a rack on one side, where several spare leather aprons were hanging.

After that, Thomas started going to the forge a couple of times a week. He was more careful not to work too late after his first experience. He wasn't entirely sure why he was even going. It wasn't part of his duties, and it didn't earn him anything but sore muscles. Grom rarely spoke, and when he did, it was usually to give simple instructions. Even so, Thomas kept returning, and an unspoken friendship grew between him and the dwarf. Eventually, he learned that Grom was only thirty-two years of age, and while this seemed quite old to Thomas, it was apparently very young for a dwarf.

"What's that face for? We're nearly the same age!" Grom's gruff voice held a chuckle.

"How's that nearly the same age? You're eighteen years older than me!" replied Thomas curiously.

"Think of it this way, you're twelve, so in just six years, ye'll be of age. I'll be thirty-eight, and by dwarven reckoning, I'll still have two years before I reach majority."

Thomas mused on that for a while, "So, in a sense, we're almost the same age?"

"Aye." Grom's eyes held a lively twinkle. "Right now, I'm bigger an' older lookin', but by the time you get grown I'll still be a teenager, if dwarves used that term. Hell, I didn't even pick up me first hammer 'til I was past twenty!"

"Why did you leave home?" As soon as he asked, Thomas wondered if he had presumed too much. He didn't mean to make Grom uncomfortable, but it was too late now.

Grom's face grew thoughtful as he chewed over the question, "I suppose I didn't agree with some things that I was taught. You know most dwarves worship Dramig, right?"

Thomas nodded and the dwarf continued, "Well Dramig is a bit different than Delwyn."

"But he's a good god too. The brothers say that he helped Delwyn when she fought Gravon." Thomas wasn't sure what else to say, so he trailed off into silence.

"Aye he is," Grom replied, "But there's one particular difference that's important to me."

"Well Dramig created the earth, and Delwyn the sun." For some reason, Thomas knew his remark wasn't anywhere close to the point.

"Dramig is very concerned with the law, and most dwarves live by it, there's right, and there's wrong. My people don't see much in between. They don't see much reason for second chances. Delwyn's followers believe in redemption, and for redemption to have a place, they set much store in mercy, if there's any hope of redemption. Mercy is what brought me here, and redemption is what keeps me." Grom's deep baritone grew silent.

"Did something happen to cause you to leave?" asked Thomas.

"Aye." The simple reply made it clear Grom wasn't going to speak further on that topic, and his face held an expression that made Thomas feel bad for asking.

Thomas let the subject drop that day, and he had no more opportunities to question Grom that week, or the week after. His classes kept him busy, and Brother Simon seemed to enjoy giving them writing assignments in the evenings. One particular assignment caused him a bit of trouble.

The essay was supposed to be about the sealing of Gravon, a time when the gods fought together to seal the Devouring Beast in his eternal prison. Thomas felt fairly confident about it, since Sarah had told him the story herself, and he remembered it quite well. As a consequence, he didn't actually pay much attention to the reading they were given to write their essay from.

He arrived to class on time, and things went well from there, until the boys were asked to read their essays. He was rather nervous about reading in front of the class, but luckily Ivan was called first. *Whatever that idiot wrote, mine will look better by comparison,* he thought to himself, but as Ivan read his essay he found himself surprised by the content. Several parts of the story seemed to be missing, nothing too important, but the ending bothered him.

After he finished, Brother Simon made Ivan wait for a moment. "Does anyone have any comments before we continue?"

Something warned Thomas that this wasn't the time to bring up his questions, but for once he ignored his good sense. "Why did you leave out the part involving Anteriolus?" he asked. The class got quiet for a moment as all eyes turned to him. Thomas felt uncomfortable mentioning the Prince of Darkness, but his part in the story had been completely omitted.

"What do you mean?" Ivan was clearly confused.

"You said that Delwyn defeated Gravon and cast him down into the Pit, where she sealed him away for all eternity, but that's not completely true. She didn't defeat him completely, she just temporarily overpowered him, and she didn't seal him, Anteriolus did, and has the key to Gravon's prison to this day." Thomas could feel the other boys gaping stares, as if he'd just grown fins and tried to swim in the middle of the classroom.

"Are you daft, or just trying to make a fool of yourself? There's nothing like that in the reading assignment." Ivan was sneering now; the disbelief on the other boys' faces told him he had the upper hand. He was about to move onto a scathing remark about stray dogs in class when Brother Simon interrupted.

"Where did you learn that?" The man's voice was quiet but stern.

Now Thomas knew he was on shaky ground, "Well sir—before I came to the temple, a friend told me the stories, and she seemed very sure of the details."

"And who was your friend?" Brother Simon seemed genuinely curious, rather than angry.

"Sarah was an orphan, but she was the one who directed me to the temple when I had...," Thomas stopped himself, he'd been about to say, 'when I had nowhere else to go' but he knew that would only earn him more ridicule. "She knew a lot about history and the gods," he finished, feeling a bit foolish.

"Did she think she was royalty too?" Ivan's scorn was etched on his face. "Maybe she thought she was the queen of dogs."

"No, she wouldn't let anyone address her as royalty, but she seemed...," Thomas caught himself. He'd been about to describe her to Ivan. The very thought made him ill as he considered what Ivan would do with her memory if he gave him any more information.

"Ivan, please sit down, your behavior isn't what we like to encourage here," said Brother Simon.

The priest paused while Ivan took his seat, before continuing, "As a matter of fact, Thomas' orphan friend was right; although it surprises me she would know these things. Those details are normally reserved for later training after entering the clergy, they aren't common knowledge."

That got everyone's attention. The mocking grins turned into confused looks. The moment passed quickly though. Brother Simon ended the class early and took up the rest of the papers. When he took Thomas', he looked at it thoughtfully before returning to his desk. He was still reading it as Thomas filed out with the other students.

Father Whitmire heard a light knock on his study door. The hour was late, but it wasn't unusual for some of the brothers to call on him for advice in the evening. He frequently worked late hours anyway. Looking up he spoke in a firm tone, "Come in."

Poking his head around the door Brother Simon looked in, "Are you busy Father? If so, I can come back later."

"No, no, come on in, I was just signing off on some reports." The older priest's expression was open as he tried to put the younger man at ease, "You seem like you have something on your mind."

"Well, yes, it concerns young Thomas, the boy you brought to the temple a few years ago." Brother Simon paused looking at the older man, but Father Whitmire didn't seem inclined to interrupt, instead lifting one eyebrow as if to indicate Simon should get on with it. "It seems Thomas has had some prior instruction in religious history, including some things that are not common knowledge outside of clerical circles." Gaining momentum, he went on to relate the story of the students' essays. "I find it hard to credit his tale of learning it from an orphan girl." At last Simon had run out of things to say and waited to see what his superior would say.

While listening, Father Whitmire had taken a thoughtful pose, steepling his fingers and closing his eyes. Opening them, he gazed at Simon intently, "I'm going to show you something. I'd like to know what you think of it, but please remember this is in strictest confidence. Only the inner council has seen this." He stared at Simon, waiting.

"Of course, Father."

Moving to a cabinet, Whitmire rifled through several folders until he found what he was looking for, a large square sheet of paper with something drawn on it. Careful not to crease it, he brought it to the desk and laid it flat, motioning Simon over to look. "What do you make of that?"

At first Simon had no idea; it appeared to be a rough sketch of the symbol of Delwyn. What confused him was that it had a rough outline of a human chest drawn around it, as though someone had confused an anatomy textbook with a religious document. "I'm not sure of the context... is this a drawing of a symbol or someone...?"

"Both, it's a drawing of Thomas' chest that I made myself the night I brought him to the temple," said the elder priest. He watched Simon carefully, gauging his reaction.

"Why did you draw our Lady's symbol upon it?"

"Because that's what's on his chest, a scar-like birthmark, which bears exact resemblance to the symbol of our order," explained Whitmire.

"Everyone thought you brought him in out of pity, an act of random kindness, but this!" Brother Simon was flustered and excited. "You didn't just save a random boy; this is a sign from the goddess herself!"

"I didn't save him at all, quite the reverse actually," with that he began to relate his own story, and his own shame. Sometimes honesty in her service was a hard choice, but since that night Father Whitmire had decided never to shirk his duty again.

After a week, the commotion surrounding Thomas and his 'orphan girl' died down a bit. Particularly refreshing was the way Brother Simon treated him now. The young man was careful to keep an eye on Thomas and frequently intervened whenever he saw Ivan causing him trouble. Of course, this merely served to intensify Ivan's dislike of him, but Thomas didn't mind that at all. He was doing well in his classes and beginning to realize that he wouldn't be a student forever. Such thoughts led him to ponder what path he should choose for the future.

While Thomas enjoyed working at the forge with Grom now and then, he didn't think he had it in him to be a good smith. The boys had also lately begun light training in arms and armor, which could lead to a military career or service with the paladins of Delwyn. Somehow Thomas couldn't really picture himself spending his life as a warrior, though.

Lost in thought he found himself at Grom's forge yet again. Luckily the dwarf was close to the end of a long project. Finishing that left the stoic dwarf in a good mood, and of a mind to chat, which was an infrequent occurrence.

After discussing Grom's plan for his next project Thomas figured he might be ok in asking a few more personal questions, "How long have you lived in Port Weston?"

"'Bout five years," Grom's tone was light.

"What did you do before you came here?"

"Wandered around a bit. I had some money, so I just took things as they came for a while, a'fore I found Port Weston and decided to try makin' a living smithing here."

Emboldened by Grom's easy words, Thomas figured he could keep going, "Why did you come to the temple to smith, wouldn't you make more on your own?"

Grom grimaced, "Aye." His simple reply made Thomas sure that would probably be the end of the conversation, but after a moment's thought Grom continued, "I had enough when I got to Port Weston, and I did set up a smithy. None of the smith's in town would take me on, probably fearful I'd drive away customers, or outshine them. Even at that age I had more skill and experience than most of the smiths here in town." Grom paused. "I set up my own place. Despite their rules, I was able to pass the master's test here, and I had the coin to buy tools. Things went pretty well for a year or so, until that business with Alec."

"Who's Alec?" Thomas had a good idea, but he wanted to hear the story from Grom's perspective.

"Ahh, ye wouldn't know about that would ye?" Grom's face took on a pained expression. "Well there was a young lad, son of one of the merchants, he took up hangin' around the smithy, sorta like you have. But Alec had problems. He didn't get along with his father, maybe that's why he hung around, since we had a bit in common that way. He made a lot of talk of leavin' home, strikin' out on his own. I think I might've been a bad example for him. He was always a bit too interested in hearing how I'd run off on me own."

"Doesn't sound like you did anything wrong," Thomas put in.

"Tell that to the magistrate. A few months after I met Alec, he up and run off. Naturally, his parents blamed me. Accused me of spiriting him off, or even killing him and hiding the body. Some nasty rumors got started after that," Grom sighed and took a deep breath.

"Anyway, the magistrate was all set to send me off as a menial to the mining camp. They didn't have a body so they couldn't charge me with murder, but still, five years workin' as a near slave didn't appeal to me none. That was when Father Whitmire intervened."

"Father Whitmire?" The mention of his benefactor's name piqued Thomas' interest.

"Yeah, he knew they were givin' me a bad deal, mostly just because they didn't like me beard and short stature. So, he talked the magistrate into giving me parole, in custody of the temple. And here I've been, the past few years, smithing for the temple. Still got a couple of years left before me parole's done." Remembering their previous conversation, Grom's words made more sense now. *Mercy is what brought me here, and redemption is what keeps me.* Thomas was not sure that what Grom had said before referred to just this incident though, in fact he had a feeling there was more.

"Did they ever find Alec?" The conversation had grown dark, and Thomas was hoping to find a way to switch topics.

"Aye, they found him. Two towns over, got drunk and hung himself. When word got back, Father Whitmire tried to have my sentence removed, but the magistrate wouldn't hear of it. Said I'd probably urged him to it. He only agreed to clear my record once the parole is done. Right old bastard he is. Makes me no mind anyway, the food's good here, plenty of work, and the priests are better than most humans."

"You like smithing don't you?"

"Aye, it's in me blood."

"So, this is what you were looking for when you left home then, a place to craft among decent people?" Thomas felt better thinking perhaps Grom's story had a bit of a happy ending.

Grom raised a bushy eyebrow, "I thought so, but all this talkin' has me to thinking perhaps I judged me Dad a bit more harshly than I should've."

"What do you mean?" asked Thomas.

"I come from warrior stock; the axe is in me blood as much as the hammer, though I've forsaken it since I left home."

"Why?" Thomas was getting confused, but felt certain there was some deep meaning.

"Mercy. There was no mercy for foes at home, be they dwarf or orc. 'Twas only the hard rules of iron. But here, here maybe I can temper the axe's edge." Left unspoken were the words, *with mercy.*

CHAPTER 4
PUNISHMENT

A few days later Thomas' routine was interrupted when he was called out of his first class to report to Father Whitmire's office. Ordinarily this wouldn't have bothered him too much, but it was odd to be called out of class. As he walked out Ivan caught his eye and gave him a knowing smile, which made him wonder what the other boy knew.

Stepping into the hallway he was surprised to find one of the temple paladins. Dressed in full armor and carrying a scimitar, he cut an intimidating figure. Thomas didn't even know his name. Without a word the man fell in beside him and walked with him to the high priest's office. He had the distinct impression that he was being escorted. Once he arrived he knocked once, and then hearing a voice he entered the room.

Father Whitmire looked up, his expression was grim, "I see you're here. Thomas listen to me carefully." His voice had a strange edge to it, as though each word were deadly serious.

"Yes sir," said Thomas somberly.

"In a few minutes that door will open again and you will be escorted to the justice chamber. Don't argue, don't question, just do as you're told and keep your mouth shut. When you get to the chamber they'll take you in, and you'll meet Father Tremmond, he will be presiding over the hearing..."

"But what's going on?" Thomas interjected.

"I'm not allowed to discuss it with you beforehand. Now pay attention." His eyes made it clear that he wouldn't entertain any more questions. "Speak only when spoken to, answer any question put to you truthfully and without dawdling. Do not volunteer anything," finished, the high priest rose and left the room without looking back.

Sitting in the room, Thomas felt incredibly alone. He knew something terrible had happened, and he had a suspicion that for some reason blame was about to fall squarely on his shoulders. He remembered the look on Ivan's face as he left the classroom. *What does he know? What do they think I did?* For a moment, he was paralyzed by the thought. In his life prior to the temple he had often been accused of things, usually theft of food. In every case, whether guilty or not, he'd been soundly thrashed. *If they got their hands on me.*

As he sat cudgeling his brain for an answer he thought of Grom's story, how he'd been falsely accused of killing a young man. Panic rose in his mind, and he fought to stay calm. If he was blamed for something like that, what would happen to him? Would he be cast out? Sent to the town jail? His mind was spinning with ever more fantastic and terrifying thoughts, until at last it went blank.

Relax. In his mind, he could hear Sarah's voice, full of confidence as it ever was. *You shall ever be sheltered by us and given succor in time of need.* Was that a memory?

Or had he really heard her speaking those words again? Thomas felt sure he was beginning to lose his mind. He shook his head, as if to clear it, but nevertheless he felt much calmer now. "I'm a fool," he said to himself, "in trouble up to my ears, and my first thought is that a girl not much older than myself is gonna come and save me. And now I'm talking to myself as well."

About then the paladin from before opened the door, "It is time, please come with me."

Thomas rose and followed him along the corridor to the temple's small justice chamber. The room was rarely used and was sparsely appointed, housing a small desk and a couple of chairs. The accused was expected to stand throughout the proceedings. As he entered the room Thomas felt the tingle of magic on his face. A strange compulsion began to take hold, and he knew that it meant to bind his tongue, forcing him to speak nothing but the truth. Wordlessly he resisted, and after a moment he felt the tingle fade away.

Father Tremmond sat behind the desk and held an air of gravity about him. He wasted no time getting to the matter at hand, "As some of you are aware, we are here today to address a matter of theft. In particular, the theft of the silver censer and candlesticks used at the ancillary altar. Brother Jenkins if you would give us the details surrounding their disappearance."

Brother Jenkins was a small man, neat in appearance as always. Thomas had rarely heard him speak other than during the morning services. "The censer was last used yesterday, at the dawn awakening." The dawn awakening was the name of their morning ritual to honor the sun. "Afterwards I put them in the chest at the base of the altar as a matter of habit. Although I didn't make note of it at the time, I'm fairly certain the candlesticks were in their places then as well. I would have noticed had they been absent."

Tremmond spoke, "Did you use them again after that point?"

"No sir, I didn't. The next time I saw them was when we recovered them from Thomas' cell," answered Jenkins. His words brought a shocked look to Thomas' face, his worst fears were coming to pass.

"Where were they located in his cell?"

"They were clumsily hidden, beneath his mattress."

"How much would these items be valued at, on the common market?" continued Tremmond.

"I'm not sure, but our cost to replace them would likely run to more than forty gold," responded the priest.

"Thank you, Brother Jenkins, your testimony was most insightful," Father Tremmond took a deep breath, preparing to continue...

"Why did you search my room? Does my poverty make me automatically suspect?!" Thomas felt his fear replaced by a low anger. Even as he spoke he could see Father Whitmire frowning at him, warning him to silence.

"Young man you will remain silent until addressed, or I will cut the proceedings short and move straight to the punitive phase." Tremmond's voice was calm, but contained an undercurrent of hard steel. "Now if we may continue, Brother Simon step forward."

Thomas' teacher stepped up, "If it please you, I will answer all questions as truthfully as possible."

"You were put in charge of the search were you not?"

"Yes, your honor."

"For the benefit of the accused will you explain why?" Tremmond stared at Thomas as he said this.

"By temple policy the first place searched after any theft within the grounds is the student's dormitory. Since I am their house master, I generally lead the searches there in these cases."

"Was Thomas' room the first you searched?"

"No, your honor, being on the second floor it was probably around the twentieth or so, I didn't count." Brother Simon looked distinctly uncomfortable.

"Thank you, Brother, you may return to your place." Simon stepped back and Father Tremmond continued, "Thomas, this court will now question you, but before we continue I must warn you that this chamber is under a spell to prevent falsehoods. Any attempt to commit perjury will meet with failure and only make your position worse."

"Begging your pardon sir, the spell didn't take hold, not that I would lie anyway," Thomas felt sure that the priests would know their magic hadn't worked either way.

"You realize that your admission casts doubt on any testimony you give from this point?" Father Tremmond seemed genuinely puzzled.

Father Whitmire broke in, "It should also serve to reinforce the lad's reputation for honesty."

Tremmond glared at the abbot, "Your grace, although you hold the esteemed position of abbot over our temple, may I remind you that I am in charge of this court? Any further interruptions are likely to hurt his case despite your good intentions."

The elder priest barely concealed his anger as he tried to hold his tongue, "Of course, you are correct your honor, please pardon my remark, I merely wished to remind the court that Thomas has been a model student in past."

"I will keep that in mind before making any decisions, now if you don't mind?" Father Tremmond could make a career out of looking annoyed.

"Thomas, did you steal the censer and candlesticks in question?'

"No sir," Thomas had a sinking feeling that nothing he said would make a difference.

"Do you know how the items came to be in your room?"

"No sir."

"You realize that without some better evidence I will be forced to find you guilty?" For a moment, the priest turned judge seemed almost sympathetic.

"Yes sir, unfortunately I have no defense to offer other than my character, and given the circumstances that seems like it won't be enough to satisfy anyone." Thomas met the judge's eyes squarely, refusing to act the part of a criminal.

"The sentence for theft of temple property, by any member of the temple, is expulsion. After which you will be remanded to the city authorities for low justice. If there is no further evidence or commentary, I will proceed with..." A loud noise broke the silence and some shouting could be heard from the hallway outside.

"Wait! Wait! Let me get me say!" Standing in the door was an angry dwarf. Grom appeared to have been running, and still wore his leather apron. *He must have heard and come straight from his work.* Thomas winced inwardly, knowing that it would not help Grom's own standing at the temple, if he annoyed the temple justicer.

The paladin guarding the room seemed unsure what to make of the intrusion. Moving forward he looked ready to deal with Grom in a forceful fashion. "Let him speak!" This came from Father Whitmire, and the guard stopped, uncertain.

"Let him in, we'll hear his words." Father Tremmond remained calm despite the tension in the room. Brushing a bit of soot from his apron, Grom moved forward.

"Yer honor I saw another student entering Thomas' room last night." The short statement stopped everyone in their tracks.

"When did you see this?"

"Early this morning, the first bell after midnight." Calm now, the dwarf kept his words simple and straightforward.

"Did you recognize this student?"

"Yes sir, 'twas Ivan, and a right scoundrel he is," he couldn't hide his poor opinion of the other boy, so he didn't even try.

"You didn't have any difficulty picking out his features in a darkened corridor? The lights would have been out long before this." Tremmond was careful in his questioning.

"Beggin' your pardon your honor, my people live under the ground, a darkened corridor is nearly as bright to me as daytime is to you. It was no trouble to see the rogue's face, though I doubt me that he noticed me."

"Why do you say that?"

"Cuz if he had, he'd have run off without attempting his bit of skullduggery," Grom showed some satisfaction at that.

"How did you come to be following a student about the dormitory at that late hour?" The priest was clearly suspicious.

"I live on that floor yer honor." The dwarf remained calm, although inwardly he was beginning to worry at the direction the questions were leading.

"And what caused you to be in the hallway at that hour, Master Dwarf?"

"I was returnin' from a small errand when I saw Ivan climbin' over the outside wall." Grom could have lied, but he wasn't about to taint his story with a fabrication now.

"You saw this from the dormitory?" The tension in the room had risen, and Tremmond had raised an eyebrow with this question.

"No sir, I saw it from the street outside. After that I kept me distance and followed him back to the dormitory. At the time I figger'd he was just up to some schoolboy prank." A trickle of sweat ran down the dwarf's temple, leaving the temple grounds at night was a violation of his parole. In fact, he had gone to give money to Alec's mother, something he had done anonymously several times in the past. But he wasn't about to dishonor her by admitting this.

"For what reason did you leave the temple grounds?" Tremmond was well aware of the terms of Grom's parole.

"That I cannot say sir, but to assure you it was for no evil deed. I felt it was necessary, or I'd not have taken the risk, but I felt I had to make good on a debt to a friend." Inwardly Grom resigned himself, with his admission he'd as good as sentenced himself to five years' labor at the mines.

"Grom, you know of the conditions of your parole. You must also be aware that should you abrogate those conditions, you may be held to the full penalty you were given by the city magistrate. Of more concern to me is the fact that the temple would face a loss of the monies paid to secure your parole. Does none of this concern you in the least?" The priest's voice was rising in volume and stridence as he spoke.

"Yes sir, it does. The temple has been good to me. I have no excuse but to say I am prepared to accept the result of my action. I made a choice and I'll stand..."

"You put the reputation of this temple and the good men and women who took you in at stake! I could have you turned over to the magistrate now, to face the consequences!" Thomas' heart sank at those words, but then Tremmond's face softened slightly. "Still, it has not escaped our notice that your sentence was unjustly given. Therefore, we will give you a choice: you may accept three lashes tomorrow at noon, before the eyes of everyone at this temple, in payment for the shame you nearly brought upon us, or you will be remanded to the magistrate to serve your full sentence. How choose you, master dwarf?" A hush had fallen over the room.

Grom's head had dipped a bit while listening to the justice's speech, but as he spoke he lifted his chin and met the man's eyes proudly, "I'll be takin' the lashes yer honor, and glad fer yer mercy."

This was too much for Thomas, "No! You can't do that, it's not fair!" The words burst out, but Father Whitmire was already beside him and laid his hand on the boy's shoulder.

"Please remove them from the courtroom. We'll take a short recess while Ivan is summoned to make an accounting." Thomas found himself being ushered from the room.

Chapter 5
The Hidden Sun

The morning moved with agonizing slowness. The dawn had come brightly, as it often did, cheerful and full of sunshine and birdsong. Yet Thomas felt at odds with the weather, today was no day for clear skies and warm sun. Today his friend was to be whipped, in part for defending him.

Ivan had been expelled the day before. He would have received lashes as well, for theft and his attempt to destroy Thomas' reputation, but his father had paid a fine of two-hundred gold to avoid shame to the family. Thomas got no joy from that however, he hadn't really hated Ivan to begin with. That the young nobleman had felt enough ill will to actually try to get Thomas whipped and expelled left him confused. In any event, he couldn't get past his own feeling of dread knowing Grom would be receiving lashes, for what seemed a harmless act.

In spite of the way time dragged, noon arrived, and all too soon. The main courtyard slowly filled with people as the entire temple populace turned out for Grom's punishment. Thomas was amazed that so many people lived and worked there, for he had never seen them gathered all at once. A man stood by the post in the center of the yard. He had never paid much attention to it before, but now he noticed the large iron nail protruding at the top, presumably to attach the manacles of those to be punished. The man holding the whip was one of the temple guards, but Thomas didn't recognize him.

A few minutes before noon Grom walked out, unescorted. Trailing behind him were two guards, but they seemed unnecessary. The dwarf proudly approached the post, unfettered and unforced. He stepped up to the post and looked squarely in the eye of the man that held the whip, "Good mornin'"

"If you'll remove your shirt please, and we'll need to bind your wrists to keep you in place." The guard seemed almost deferential; the story of Grom's testimony had already made its rounds in the guard house. Without intending it, Grom had won the respect of more than a few guards for his fearless testimony. Indeed, it would have been hard to find anyone in the courtyard that day who truly felt Grom's punishment was deserved. Nonetheless, it was unavoidable.

"Nah nah... let me do this me own way, an if you need to bind me I'll gladly take a fourth stroke." So saying, the dwarf removed his shirt and wound it into a tight cord, wrapping it around his hands he put the middle over the nail. With his back facing the crowd, Thomas was surprised to see a few silver lines across the broad dwarven shoulders. *This isn't his first time to be whipped. Could that have been from his time before he left home?* As usual, more questions than answers went through Thomas' mind.

The whip uncoiled like a deadly snake, graceful almost, as it swung back, before it came forward again.

Slicing through the air it struck Grom's back with an ugly sound, leaving a long line across his back with blood welling up. On the second stroke droplets of blood flew out, and Grom's body convulsed, his hands gripping his shirt as his knees buckled for a moment. Straightening back up, Thomas could see his face had gone ash white, but the proud expression on his face was still there.

The third stroke came after a brief pause, which made it seem even crueler. As it landed a small grunt escaped the dwarf's lips while his body strained to remain in place. Although his lashes were done, he didn't move for a minute or more, taking deep breaths, Grom's muscles were locked, and it seemed to take him a while to relax enough to release his shirt and step away.

A cloud passed over the sun, hiding its face, as though the goddess herself were ashamed to see what had happened. In the sudden gloom Thomas noticed a familiar face at the front of the crowd. A face he had never expected to see again. Quietly moving forward, Sarah approached Grom, ignoring the guards on either side. If one were to look closely, a bright red droplet of blood stood out on her cheek, a memento of the dwarf's pain.

Thomas himself was utterly surprised to see her there. She looked just the same as she had two years before. Small, thin, a ragged shift covered her body. Stopping a foot from Grom, he could see tears welling in her eyes, spilling over to trace silent tracks down her smudged cheeks.

The sky grew even darker as the thin girl moved up beside the dwarf. Their bodies were a study in stark contrasts. Lithe to the point of being too thin, the girl looked incredibly frail next to the broad muscular form of the dwarf, even though she was slightly taller. Reaching up her hand traced a bloody line across his back, blood smearing across her pale hand.

Transfixed, Thomas was unable to comprehend what he was seeing. The world had gone dark, with the only light seeming to radiate softly from the girl and her red-gold hair. Looking about, Thomas realized he was the only one left standing, everyone else in the courtyard from the eldest of priests to the smallest of children had fallen to their knees, heads bowed; some were openly crying. Sarah looked over the crowd and opened her mouth to speak.

"You should be ashamed!" Her anger lashed the crowd like a physical blow. "You have taken one innocent of wrongdoing, and this is how you treat him? When did my house become a temple honoring pain? When did my house become a home for injustice? This is *not* what I have taught!"

Father Tremmond finally spoke up, lifting his head, "Lady, I sought only to keep the law. Please forgive these people, for they have done no wrong."

"An' now ye know me. You whose arrogance blinded you! Now you know humility, after blood has been spilled. As I have darkened the sky, now I darken your eyes, that you may see the light better. Remember this day." At that point Father Tremmond's eyes glazed over with a fine haze. "Your words are spoken fairly, but everyone here will remember this day with shame, for you are all guilty in some part."

Reaching out liquid gold spilled from her bloodied hand, washing over Grom's torn skin, and where it passed over the skin was left smooth and unblemished. Falling to his knees at last, Grom thanked her and begged her forgiveness for the people present. "I know ye not lass, but if you are the Morningflower I beg you to show mercy today. These folk have given me far more than the hurt I received. They are not perfect, nor am I, but their hearts are mainly kind, and they worship you as best they can, despite their flaws."

Looking deeply into Grom's dark eyes, Sarah smiled, and with her smile the sun emerged, returning light and warmth to the courtyard. "You do not know me, son of the earth, but your heart is true. You have my blessing, though in time you may come to rue it. Even I cannot protect you from the sorrows the future will bring."

Thomas, still standing, made as if to speak, but as soon as his mouth opened time froze in place. *Don't Thomas. This is not the time. If I answer your questions now it might lead to the blight of all creation. Be at peace, and remember that time.*

She was gone. Time snapped back into place, and Thomas found himself with tears in his eyes. The sun shone down with such brilliance he felt blinded, and quietly he sank to his knees to join the others in silent prayer.

It was some days before things returned to normal. The temple was ablaze with talk each day as everyone shared their story of the event. Of particular interest, was the fact that most saw something entirely different from what Thomas had seen. Where he had seen an orphan girl, with wild unkempt hair, most had witnessed Delwyn in all her glory, wielding a flaming sword in one hand, and holding the sun in the other. That day had taught them humility, but it also gave them new hope, for they knew the Morningflower was still active, still vigilant, and still cared, despite the hard realities of life.

Even more curious, the next week Grom presented himself to Father Whitmire, asking to be entered into the rolls as one of Delwyn's followers. He was the first child of Dramig to do so in more than a generation, and dwarves have very long generations.

A woman walked the street, alone and without purpose. Passersby, had they looked at her, would have been taken by her beauty. Ruffled and weary she held an air about her that would give any man pause. Her raven hair was tied back, and her clothes, while worn and travel stained were of a quality that hinted at money. Pale skin offset her black hair, and made her blue eyes seem to blaze, like icy jewels.

Evening had stolen upon her, and the light was fading quickly. The infrequent streetlamps assured that Islana would soon have difficulty finding her way in the dark. Storm clouds were threatening, and she knew she needed to find shelter soon, before the inns shuttered windows and barred their doors. Few would let a stranger in at night with a storm brewing.

She quickened her step as she scanned the street ahead. A cold gust sent a chill down her neck, and she drew her collar closer. As she walked, she kept her eyes moving, watching the alleyways as she passed. A woman alone could not afford carelessness; watching Franz die had taught her that.

A dark lump in the alley to her left caught her attention. She kept walking even as her mind sorted over what she had seen. *Was that a dog on the ground? A person? It was too small to be an adult, a child perhaps?* Commonsense bade her to keep moving regardless. *That had to be a child.* She stopped. The harsh realities of life had taught her to avoid getting involved in things that didn't concern her, but inside she was still a compassionate woman. *Damn it!*

Turning she returned to the alley way, cautiously approaching the odd bundle. A lock of blond hair spilled out onto the ground at one end. Before her hand reached the rough blanket, she knew it was a child. Tugging the edge of the blanket she saw the face of a small boy. Blue lips made his plight clear, the child was freezing to death. *It's a miracle he's still breathing now.* She knew there was very little time. Carefully, she lifted the child from the ground, cradling his head. He weighed surprisingly little, and could not have been more than three or four years of age.

Holding the child firmly she broke into a careful jog. Fortunately, she'd always been athletic, and her strong legs carried her quickly down the road. The shops on either side of the narrow street were already closed, but ahead she could see a church. She recognized the familiar design, her family venerated Badon, and all of his buildings shared a similar form. With renewed vigor, she hurried to the main gate.

Of course, it was locked as well, but she knew someone had to be on duty within. After pounding on the door for several minutes a small window in the door opened. "Stop your pounding! What do you want?" The voice that issued forth sounded annoyed.

"I need your help, I have a small child, he's freezing. Please let me in...," she tried to keep her voice calm, but the urgency was clear.

"Go home, the temple is closed for the night."

"I am from another town, please you have to help me, I found this child in the street."

"Do you have payment?" She could see an old man's face peering at her.

"What? No! I just got here, this isn't even my child! Are you going to help him or not?" she asked.

The small window closed with a snap. For a moment Islana stared at it in shock, until finally a red rage grew inside her. All the injustice she had witnessed, at home and on the road, built within her, until the storm within seemed greater than the one brewing in the skies above.

A small cough broke her from her violent reverie. The sound was weak, almost pathetic, not the cough of a child struggling to recover. The sound was more reminiscent of someone's dying gasp. *He's going to die! Right here in my arms, just feet from help.* The child's hands were icy in her grip and a sense of hopelessness swept over her.

"It's ok little one, it's ok..," she spoke softly, as if talking to an infant, as much to reassure herself as the child. Reaching down she pulled out her long knife, the only weapon she had on her. Trying not to think of what she was doing to her only clothes, she cut a ragged gash in her tunic and undershirt, from neck to waist. The wind was quick to take advantage, causing her to gasp for a moment as the cold air hit her bare skin. Working as quickly as she could, she unbundled the small boy and carefully put him against her chest. It was like placing a cold stone there. Wrapping his blanket around her mid-section she tied him in place there against her belly, hoping it would be enough to warm him.

The next hour was a cold misery. As if to further her torment the sky opened up and began to rain. The cold water slowly seeped through her cloak, leaving her wet and shivering before long. She went from door to door, trying each one. None were open, few bothered even to answer her pleas, but she refused to give up.

At last she came to a large wooden door, carved with symbols of the Morningflower. Not daring to hope, she began ringing the bell that hung next to the door. Moments later, she heard a deep voice from the other side. "Aye, I hear ye, hold yer horses!" A face appeared in the door's small window. Coarse features and a very hairy face looked through the window. Whoever it was seemed to be stretching to reach the window, his lower face and chin were completely hidden.

"Hmph! Are ye daft lassie? It's pouring down tonight!" Granite eyes swept over her, capturing the scene. Suddenly he was gone, and she heard the bolt draw back. The door opened and standing there was the shortest, broadest man she had ever seen. Clad in a leather hauberk, his beard was impressive beyond belief. "Get inside! You'll freeze yer tits off girl!" His gruff voice brought her back to the present. Too tired to be angry at his rough remark she moved into the warm foyer. After the biting wind outside it felt like a furnace, albeit a welcome one.

"I found this child, he's half frozen, I fear he will...," she began.

He cut her off, "Hang on, let me get someone." As he spoke, an elderly man walked in.

"What's all the fuss?" The man's bushy eyebrows went up as he noticed Islana. "Over here girl, let's get you warmed up, and let me see the boy." Ushering her into another room he helped her onto a soft pallet. Most likely a sleeping place for the door guard.

Islana removed her cloak, grateful to be rid of its sodden weight. Unwrapping the blanket, she drew the boy out and laid him near the fire. His breathing seemed unsteady, but he was noticeably warmer after his time bundled against her. A weak cough rose from his thin blue lips.

"We've got to get him undressed, those wet clothes are only making things worse." The old man began removing the boy's coarse tunic and rubbing his hands to help warm them. At this point Islana became aware of another presence in the room. The dwarf was talking to a young man. He was dressed in a simple brown robe, but something about him drew her eyes. Her stare caught his attention, and he met her gaze with warm brown eyes. A second later he ducked out of the room.

Turning back to the child, she was relieved to see that he was still breathing. The old man had wrapped him in a warm blanket and was now looking over at her. "Will he be all right?" she asked.

"I'm not sure, the Abbot is out at the moment, and none of our better healers are here at present. We'll do the best we can and trust the goddess." The old man's eyes drifted downward. Something was odd about his expression. *What is he looking at?* She thought to herself.

Glancing down, she knew immediately. Her chest was bare and exposed, her breasts responding to the cold air in the normal fashion. A lesser woman would have panicked with embarrassment, but Islana came from a long line of noble blood. She would *not* be debased, despite her nudity. Straightening up gracefully, she ignored his stare and turned away modestly. A few choice words came to mind, but she decided to be polite instead, "Sir, if you would be so kind as to find a shirt or robe for me?"

"Miss, I think this will help." She had been looking over her shoulder at the old man when she stood up. This voice came from the other direction. In front of her stood the young man in the brown robe again, he held a large blanket toward her. His eyes were firmly fixed on her own and there was no hint of mockery in his face, just honest reassurance. He lifted the blanket to cover her nakedness. For a moment, she held his eyes, yet he never looked down. Oddly enough this made her more embarrassed than the old man's ogling. Breaking away from his gaze, she took the blanket, her cheeks flushing.

"Thomas, this child has the plague!" The old man was still examining the boy.

"What?" Islana's voice sounded too high in her own ears.

"We need Father Whitmire," said the young man. He seemed to be talking to himself.

"He's not here!" The old man seemed quite alarmed. "We've got to do something quick, or this will be all over the temple!"

"Calm down, let me fetch Sir Brevis, I'm sure he can heal this. If not, we'll find another way." Thomas looked at Islana, "Please rest, I'll be back shortly." So saying, he left the room.

After he had gone, the dwarf spoke up, "Want some food? Ye must be starved."

As a matter of fact, she was hungrier than she could ever remember being, "Yes, thank you, I appreciate the kindness."

The compliment had the desired effect, and Grom blushed slightly, "I'll get ye a bowl of stew."

In due course Thomas returned, followed by an older man. The man behind him was also dressed in a plain robe, although this one was white with red piping at the hem and sleeves. Despite his simple garb, he moved with a deadly grace. There was something about him that reminded her of a coiled spring. When he reached over to examine the boy, she noticed several fine scars crossing his forearm, and his hands were large and callused.

Kneeling, Sir Brevis bowed his head, as if in prayer. Then he brought his hands up and laid them upon the child's small form. Islana felt something, there was nothing visible, but she could feel a certain warmth suffusing the room. It was a feeling reminiscent of a mother's embrace. After a moment, he rose, and stepped back. The child's breathing was easier now, his lips a more normal pink; he appeared to be sleeping.

Sir Brevis turned, and she felt his discerning eyes watching her. "What is your name child?"

Islana felt unsure, she knew this man was of noble birth, his speech and bearing had already given that away. His tone made her feel small for a moment, as if she were in her father's house, though he had none of her father's condescension about him. "Islana, and I've already reached my majority." The words held a double meaning, first that she was no longer a child, second that she wouldn't accept being treated as one.

Brevis reached out, grasping her arm, lifting it he squeezed slightly, then moved her sleeve up to check her upper arm. She felt for all the world like a prize mare being valued for sale. "I'll not be handled like some prize!" She jerked her arm back.

"You have spirit too." Sir Brevis smiled, amused, but she mistook his meaning. Her arm came up of its own accord. Striking like a snake as she slapped Sir Brevis, or rather she would have, but his hand caught her own.

Her strength surprised him, though he wouldn't admit as much. His hand was stinging where it had caught hers. Then surprise lit his face, and a small grunt escaped his lips. Her other hand, now a fist, had struck him squarely in the midsection.

Islana's hand hurt. The man's stomach felt as though it were made of iron. Glaring at him she considered her next attack, but he released her other hand and stepped back. "Peace lady, peace, I mean you no ill will." He was laughing now. *Why is he laughing?*

She had dropped the blanket.

Snatching it up from the ground she backed away. She was properly furious now.

Sir Brevis spoke again, "I know your father." Those words brought her to a halt, and she felt a cold chill run down her spine. "Surely you heard me, Islana Eisler," he added, emphasizing the words, making sure she heard him clearly.

"How did you?" *Shut up! You're making it worse,* she inwardly berated herself. "I will take my leave now and leave the child in your care." Backing up, she retrieved her wet cloak from the floor, and her long-knife along with it. She gauged the distance to the door in case they tried to prevent her exit.

"I know much that you would do well to learn, Lady *Eisler,*" said Brevis, stressing the last word. "I know that you have been traveling alone for over a month; a noblewoman on the road without an escort. Yet you seem whole and unharmed, no small feat.

"I know that you are exceedingly strong for a woman, and your bones tell a tale of greater strength to come. I know that you took a small child from the street, and in the cold rain, you cut your fine garments up to share your warmth.

"What you need to know is this: You have come to the right house. This is a house of mercy and kindness. I do not serve your father, nor would I, were I free to do so. I serve a power far greater than any earthly lord.

"Stay here and I offer you sanctuary. Live here and you will learn what it is you seek. Your father's will has no power in this place," finished at last, Sir Brevis waited.

Islana felt foolish, she had misjudged his intentions. Worse, she had no money, no place to stay, and she had destroyed her only clothes. She'd spent the last hours in the cold, trying to save a dying child. Now she had attacked the first man to help. Her frustration was so great that it nearly brought her to tears, but her pride would not accept such weakness. "I think I've made a mistake here," she admitted.

Looking down for a moment, she thought over her options, "I accept your offer, and I'd like to apologize for my own rudeness." The words were not easy to say, but she would not owe a man anything, not even an apology.

CHAPTER 6
HUMILITY

Thomas' training had changed over the last year. Gone were the math and reading exercises, replaced with more specific instruction relating to the practices of Delwyn's faith. Many of the boys he had come to know were gone now, off to learn their trades or enter the military. The only ones left near his age were the other novitiates, those who had chosen to enter the priesthood.

The rituals and practices were interesting to Thomas, but he found that he enjoyed the meditative training more. At those times, he could almost feel Sarah's presence; it helped him to reconcile his past, with the knowledge of her true identity. He was careful to call her Delwyn during training, but inwardly, she remained Sarah to him. *If she wanted me to call her 'Delwyn' she should have introduced herself that way.* The very thought was blasphemous probably, but unlike most, he knew the goddess had a sense of humor.

As his training progressed he found himself with more free time, but Father Whitmire had planned for that fact and soon filled his spare hours with secretarial work. This provided him with a better understanding of the day to day affairs of the temple, which might have been

Whitmire's intention from the beginning. Thomas had learned not to underestimate the older man.

Sitting at a wooden desk in the Abbot's office, Thomas glanced out the window. In the yard he could see the guard and paladin candidates performing their morning exercise routine. Two figures drew his attention, as usual, that of a heavyset dwarf, and Islana's. Sir Brevis had sponsored her for training as a paladin, and after it had been established that she already possessed a solid classical education her training had moved up to martial skills and spiritual exercises.

From the occasional reports crossing Father Whitmire's desk, Thomas knew that she had already impressed her instructors. He found himself watching her run in the yard, her long black hair bound in a thick braid. She was a natural athlete, which served to reinforce her femininity rather than the opposite. Her hips moved with a sort of sinuous cadence as her legs drove her forward. In his mind's eye, Thomas merged the naked form he had glimpsed that night, with that of the woman now running below his window. He had worked hard to avoid embarrassing her, but he had seen much more than he intended, and the image kept cropping up unbidden in his mind. *What am I doing!?*

His mind snapped back into focus, and he felt a sense of guilt. *What would Sarah think of me now?* Even that thought was unfair, she was a goddess, and her priests were not forbidden to marry. Still, it felt wrong to think about other women quite that way. *Does that mean it's right to think of Sarah in that way? Of course not!* The thought had never occurred to him before, but it made him very uncomfortable, so he quickly suppressed it. He glanced at the sun, wondering if he would ever be worthy of her trust.

Islana was sweating. The morning warm-ups were followed by weapons training. Being one of only two women in the group, she felt decidedly conspicuous. It didn't help that the other girl, Kate, wasn't exactly attractive. Kate made up for her plain features with an exuberant personality, but personality didn't draw stares the way Islana's ample endowments did. To make matters worse, the excessive attention she received seemed to have created a barrier between herself and her only possible female ally.

She channeled her frustration at the situation into her reactions to the boys brave enough to approach her. Today was no exception as she stood over her fallen opponent. Walter had asked her if she would accompany him on a trip into town over the weekend. Her response had been different than usual; she'd been in a perverse mood that day, "Spar with me tomorrow, if you get the best two out of three, I'll consider it."

It didn't appear as if Walter was going to be getting up from the first bout of three. He tried to stand, but the strength had gone out of his legs. Falling over, he promptly threw up his breakfast.

"Merciful Goddess! What have you done?" Sir Brevis was shouting as he ran over. Uttering a brief prayer, he touched Walter's brow, and the boy's retching and heaving stopped.

"Islana! Did I fail to explain to you exactly what the meaning of the word *sparring* is?" He seemed completely out of sorts this morning.

"No sir," Islana stared back at him without the least bit of contrition.

"Then why are you trying to kill or maim my students?" A blood vessel on the knight's temple was pulsing as he growled the words out.

"If I was trying to kill him, he'd be dead by now," she said, arching her eyebrow without smiling. A smile would definitely have sent Sir Brevis over the edge of reason. "It isn't as though you cannot mend any hurt I give them."

"You should be aware that a blow to back of the head, such as you just delivered, can kill near instantly."

"It is also the quickest way to render someone unconscious. I was careful not to strike him that hard," she answered confidently.

The challenge in her voice was too much for Sir Brevis, "That's it! Get your gear, I'm suspending you for the rest of the week. Report to the Abbott; tell him that I want you in nothing but meditation training for the next seven days. Make sure he knows the focus should be on humility."

I just taught that lesson to Walter, why should I have to spend a week training at it? She kept that joke to herself. She knew she had crossed a line, but she wasn't sure how to correct the situation. Angry at herself more than anyone else, she picked up her things and marched back across the field.

She spent the rest of the morning sitting outside of Father Whitmire's office, waiting to be seen. Eventually Thomas appeared and ushered her into the room, a look of sympathy crossed his face before he stepped out and closed the door.

A short time later, she left the office. The abbot's words and calm demeanor had left her uncertain of herself. Thomas stood across from the doorway. She gave him a tight-lipped smile and headed toward the stairs, but rather than return to the office he fell in beside her. A questioning glance from her prompted him to speak.

"It's lunch time, if you haven't noticed." His voice was calm, without guile or subtle intentions. She liked that about him, and she supposed it was probably why she was able to relax around him. *I don't constantly feel like I'm being pursued!*

The dining hall was nearly empty; her meeting with the Abbott had put her past the usual time for lunch. The fellow serving gave them a scowl as he filled their bowls with tepid soup. She carried hers over to the small table reserved for women. Thomas sat down across from her.

Most men would have been too embarrassed to sit there. "Is there something I should know?" she asked. "You haven't taken up knitting, have you?"

Grinning sheepishly, Thomas looked around at the empty hall, "Would you prefer to eat alone?" He was making a joke, but the question was sincere.

"No, I'm glad for some company, it's just been a long day," she admitted.

"It's only half done. What brought you to the Abbott's door?" asked Thomas.

His tone was casual, but Islana tensed at the question. She studied his face carefully, looking for any sign that he might be mocking her. "I'm to spend the next week in nothing but meditative studies and contemplation of proper humility," she replied.

This brought more questions, and despite herself Islana shared the story of her morning on the practice field. She couldn't figure out why, but she trusted Thomas. *He's just a good listener,* she told herself.

"I just don't understand *why* I should study humility! Haven't I experienced enough humiliation in my life already? They're training me to be a warrior, not a desk clerk!" She then realized she had just insulted him. "Sorry." She looked down and quickly filled her mouth with stew before she could say anything else to offend. *I'm just full of pleasant words today.*

Glancing up she saw Thomas staring at her thoughtfully. "What?" she asked.

Thomas was considering her situation and despite her defensiveness he was thinking deeply. He met her gaze for a second, and blue eyes under locks of dark hair transfixed him for a moment, almost causing him to lose his train of thought. He smiled reflexively to cover his embarrassment before he answered, "Humiliation isn't the same as humility."

"They're looking very similar from where I'm sitting," she said sourly. She didn't really believe that, but again, her pride wouldn't let her sit silent. Thomas had a loose lock of hair drifting almost in front of his face. She resisted an urge to reach across and brush it back for him. The thought caused her to blush again, so she studied her empty bowl instead.

"Humiliation, if deliberate, is an act of aggression. It is at heart, a violent act against another's dignity. Humility is quite different," continued Thomas, his face earnest. "Humility is a gift to others, a gentleness of spirit, an expression of nobility." He paused at that, realizing he might have said too much. Rising from his seat, he excused himself, "I should be getting back."

He's so serious, I wonder if he ever laughs? Islana was seized by a moment of whimsy, "Thomas." Her voice made him stop. "Have you ever been on a picnic?"

"What?" Nothing could have surprised him as much as that question. "I'm sorry I don't understand. You asked if I had ever—I missed the last word." Surely, he had misheard her.

"A picnic...," she repeated. Islana could sense his bewilderment and knew she had him on the defensive, "...you take some food and go out to enjoy the sunshine and spring air. I thought you might be free tomorrow since there are no classes. Of course, if it seems strange to you, I suppose you could eat here instead. I'm sure the old men would miss your company." She smiled coyly. *I'm flirting! What the hell is wrong with me? What would Franz think?* She started to retract her offer.

"Sure," said Thomas, fighting down a surge of panic.

"Meet me in the northern courtyard tomorrow, I know just the spot." Jumping up, she took her bowl and left before he could say anything else. Glancing back, she saw him still standing where she had left him, a curious expression on his face. Laughing inside, she headed for her room, but it was her turn to be embarrassed when she realized she had forgotten to leave her bowl. She was still carrying it and her tray when she got to her room. *There is no way I'm carrying this back there right now.*

Closing the door to her room, she sat down on the bed. *Did I just arrange an assignation? With a novitiate priest?* Moaning to herself, she buried her head in a pillow, *Does he think it's a tryst?*

She answered herself out loud, "No Islana, you just asked a friend on a perfectly normal picnic. Why would he think that?"

Because he's male, stupid!

"Thomas isn't like that," she told herself. "He's not some rutting pig! He has far more important things on his mind, surely."

Maybe I want him to think it's a tryst. She made a decidedly unladylike yell as she threw her pillow at the far wall.

Thomas rose early the next morning. That in and of itself wasn't unusual; being a devotee of Delwyn, he was supposed to greet the dawn for his morning prayers. Waking up two hours *before* the dawn was a bit beyond the pale, even for him. He used the extra time to order his thoughts, and he prayed to Delwyn for guidance. Even though it was a casual picnic, he still felt somewhat nervous. In spite of his intent prayer and meditation, he received no answer from the goddess, although he could swear he heard Sarah's tinkling laughter. *Did I imagine that?* Considering it again, he decided it would be just like her to laugh at his situation.

The morning went slowly, and even Father Whitmire could tell he was nervous and out of sorts, though he said nothing. Finally, lunchtime arrived and Thomas made his way to the appointed spot. The northern courtyard was taken up largely by a garden, mostly vegetables. The temple tried to be as self-sufficient as possible.

One part of it was shaded by several modest apple trees. Someone had planted flowers nearby, and the overall effect was quite pleasing this time of year. Islana led him there, and he found she had already spread a large quilt on the ground. Laid out were a loaf of bread and part of a chicken, along with a small jug and some cheese.

"How did you get all this out of the kitchen?" he said wonderingly.

She smiled mischievously, "I bribed the cook, he can be most accommodating when he wants to be."

Thomas started to ask what she used for her bribe, then decided the question was indelicate, if not outright rude. "Is that water or small beer?" He preferred small beer, but wasn't picky.

"Wine."

"But..."

"Let a lady have her secrets." She had already sat down and was looking up, "Are you going to sit or just stand there all afternoon?"

Thomas sat. The food was good. It wasn't often he got to eat roast fowl, meat being a luxury seldom wasted on the novitiates. After a time, his stomach was full and he relaxed, reclining to watch the clouds as they floated by.

He had no idea what to say, and attempting to think of small talk made his mind go blank. At last Islana spoke, and began to question him about his life at the temple. Up until now she'd known little about him. She was surprised to learn that he was an orphan—

there was certainly nothing common about the way he carried himself.

He told her about his experiences since coming to the temple, but he avoided mentioning his time before that, nor did he mention his birthmark. She was quite interested to learn about Grom, and the story of the goddesses' appearance was exceptionally interesting to her. She had still been living at home then, but the story had circulated to most of the nearby towns and cities.

Eventually she felt comfortable enough to ask a few more personal questions, "Have you ever been in love, Thomas?" The question made her blush, but she was facing away so that he couldn't see her face.

"Once, I think." Sarah's image came to his mind. "I'm not entirely sure, I was a lot younger." He was completely certain, but he didn't want to sound like a fool.

She glanced at him, her nervousness replaced by curiosity, "What happened?"

"Well, as it turns out, she was well above my station. But the experience is what led me to the temple and my decision to devote myself to Delwyn." *Well above my station, what an understatement.*

"So, you lost the girl and wound up becoming a priest..." It reminded her of Franz, who had been well beneath her own rank in society. *If only he had been lucky enough to find sanctuary.* She clamped down on her next thought, she was not ready to examine that wound, it was still too tender.

"I'm not a priest, yet, just a novitiate. Don't make it sound so tragic. Priests of Delwyn may still marry after all," he kept his tone light, but inside he still felt a bit of loss over Sarah.

That broke her reverie, and she latched onto his words to stop her own sad thoughts. "Have you ever—has there been—I mean—have you met any women since then? Who made you think perhaps you might someday..." She broke off; the words 'marry' and 'love' were just too embarrassing. Especially since she realized that she wasn't asking out of disinterested curiosity, but for more personal reasons.

He was sitting up now, and she stared at his back. He paused for a moment and then answered, "No, I really haven't. There aren't that many women here, and the ones I have met so far didn't really interest me at all." His tone was casual, and he continued, trying to inject a bit more levity, "Have you met Dame Grindle? She's a sweet lady, but she's not likely to send young men off thinking of love!"

She tried to laugh, but it didn't work. The way he had responded left it clear to her that he didn't even think of her as a woman. *If I'm lucky, maybe a sister.* "Let's go, I think it might rain, I don't want to get this blanket wet." If her voice was slightly bitter, he didn't seem to notice.

"Huh? The sky is clear and the sun is out...," he began to protest.

"Just come on."

He sensed her anger, but he wasn't sure what he had done to provoke it. So, he helped her pack up and tried not to make things worse. *A beautiful woman seems interested, and I somehow make her mad.* He mentally reviewed the conversation, *I told her I wasn't interested in any other women.*

You probably mistook her intentions, he thought to himself. *She probably figured it out and decided to nip things in the bud.* At least he hadn't wound up like Walter.

CHAPTER 7
RANGER TIMON

The following week Islana avoided Thomas like the plague. For his part, he didn't make it difficult for her. He was still unsure what to say. Eventually she decided to forgive him, after all he hadn't actually done anything *wrong*. In any case, she didn't have that many friends, not enough that she could afford to lose one. Besides, she didn't really 'want' to avoid him.

When they finally spoke again they didn't talk about the picnic, nor did she invite him on any more.

A month later they were back to normal, but events got more interesting with the arrival of a ranger. That wasn't unusual in and of itself, the temple had a number of rangers associated with it. None of them lived there, at least not regularly, but one or another would stop in every few months. The rangers of Delwyn served the temple as her eyes and ears in the world beyond the city, while the priests and paladins served more directly in the cities proper.

This ranger, however, was of particular interest. Thomas had never met him personally, and he hadn't returned to the temple in almost two years, an uncommonly long time, even for those as self-reliant as the rangers were. What made his arrival even more curious was the fact that he had brought a young woman with him.

Thomas was sitting in the abbot's study when he heard a knock at the door. Crossing the room, he answered it, and found himself face to face with a tall lean man. "Can I help you sir?"

The stranger grinned at him. He had an easygoing, open face. "If you don't mind, I'm here to see Father Whitmire. I'm sure he'll want to see me." He wore dark tanned leathers and bore a sword at his side. Thomas considered how to stall him until he could inform the abbot. Then he heard a voice behind him.

"Timon! Do come in! How long has it been?"

"Nigh on two and a half years by my mark." The ranger eased past Thomas and headed for a chair by the desk. He was better looking than any man had a right to be, with long blond hair caught up in a braid.

"I'd begun to wonder if you could still keep track of time," remarked the Abbot, before turning to Thomas, "Go fetch some tea for us. Master Timon and I have a lot of catching up to do."

The priest moved back to his desk and sat down while Thomas let himself out. When he returned a few minutes later, the two were already deep in conversation. He set the tray down on the desk between them and returned to his own small writing table. Neither man paid attention to his presence, so he stayed quiet and kept his ears open.

It's not as though I'm eavesdropping. Father Whitmire would tell me if he felt I should leave the room. Still, he wasn't about to call attention to himself; the conversation was proving to be quite interesting.

"You must see some promise in her if you spent so much time on her." The older priest toyed with his spoon, a nervous habit he developed when he was trying to seem more calm than he was.

"That's one reason, among others," Timon seemed unsure how to continue. "She'd been living alone in the forest for over a year before I found her. Not something most sixteen-year olds could manage without prior training. It's safe to say I was intrigued." He looked down at his tea, the cup seemed absurdly small in his large hands, but he held it with surprising gentleness. After a moment, he continued, "Father, I have something to confess."

"Don't be so formal. We've been friends longer than I've been a priest, if you have something to tell me spit it out," said Father Whitmire. That surprised Thomas, especially since Timon didn't look *that* old.

"I trained her in woodcraft, for the better part of the past year. She was an apt pupil, possibly one of the best I've found. Perhaps because of that I let my guard down more than might be wise." The ranger was having trouble coming to the point.

"What do you mean?" the abbot was frowning.

"Living in the wild isn't much like they portray it in the stories. You hunt to survive, you bed down wherever you find a safe, dry place. The wilderness can bring out the more primal instincts, and we were in close contact for most of the year." Master Timon was staring at his cup, unable to meet Whitmire's eyes.

"So, your relationship was a bit more—physical, perhaps? Surely it was consensual? Wait don't answer that, I know you well enough to know you wouldn't force it." The priest took a deep breath. "You're old enough to know better."

Timon groaned, "I know!"

"She's barely an adult!"

"I know."

"Well so far your only crime is a lack of common sense. I'm assuming you want something of us?" Father Whitmire looked annoyed rather than angry.

"Before I ask that, let me explain a bit," said Timon. "She was with me for months before things became— complicated. In that time, she worked hard to get my 'attention'. I ignored it mostly because I thought she didn't know what she wanted. I was wrong."

"Is she in love with you?" The older man was obviously puzzled.

"No. Maybe—I'm not sure. She probably doesn't know herself. That's part of the problem." Timon set his cup down, now empty. "After she, after, well— alright a few months into things, I started to realize, that she didn't quite view human interactions in the same way most of us do. I had taught her as much as I could of the woods, but I couldn't teach her to understand her heart."

"You probably should have figured that out before you tupped her," said the priest sarcastically. Thomas had never seen him talk like this, in some ways it made him seem more human.

"I deserve that, and I wish I had. In the end, I've probably made her problem worse. Once I had gotten entangled I realized there was no possible way to train her spirit. I was serving as my own worst example."

"So I'm assuming you want the temple to train her." Whitmire phrased it as a statement.

78

"Yes, though it won't be easy. If things continue as they have she'll be nothing more than amoral, and devoid of human empathy. As it stands she currently sees men and her dealings with them in a very 'transactional' manner." Timon was embarrassed.

Father Whitmire frowned, "You as much as call her a whore."

"No! No, not yet, but I fear she's heading that way. Surely you can help her?" pleaded Timon.

Thomas was uncomfortable, he never expected such an experienced man to show such vulnerability.

"I'll do all that I can. We've been friends too long to do otherwise. Even if we weren't, I couldn't turn her away."

Timon reached out to clasp Father Whitmire's outstretched arm, "It won't be easy. She already thinks I've betrayed her by bringing her here. She must feel this is just one more example of being cast off."

Islana had been summoned to Grand Master Brevis' study. During their training exercises he was generally addressed simply as 'Sir Brevis', but his rank was quite a bit higher. It had taken a while before Islana understood the co-lateral hierarchy of the paladins. It worked out that he was in charge of not just the paladins at the temple in Port Weston, but also of the other chapter houses throughout the country.

"You called for me sir?" As her instruction had progressed she had also learned a good bit about humility and respect. The former she had gained, the latter he had earned from her.

"Our good Abbott has taken in a new ward. A young woman. She's been trained as a ranger thus far, but she will be staying at the temple a while to further her instruction in matters more spiritual." Brevis looked at her, framing his thoughts.

"I know little of woodcraft sir." She had an idea what he wanted, but her perverse nature still enjoyed drawing him out.

"Your woodcraft is entirely beside the point. As a young woman here, she is bound to feel isolated. There aren't many of the gentler sex here, and fewer still among the guard or paladins."

"Gentler sex?" queried Islana, not bothering to hide her amusement.

He snorted, "Obviously that term has never applied to you! My point is that I would like you to show her around, try to put her at ease. This is a difficult time for her."

"Do you mind if I speak freely sir?" In the past, she would have done so without bothering to ask.

"Go ahead," responded Brevis, glad that she had at least learned some protocol. He still worried, one never knew where she would go when given free rein.

"I would have done all this without instruction sir. You men over think things. We of the 'gentler sex' are quite aware of each other and very willing to help one another. It shows a lack of trust that you would have to ask, or perhaps ignorance of the workings of women." She gave him a steady look.

Sir Brevis groaned inwardly, he should have expected as much, "Is that all?"

"Yes sir," she said primly.

"Then you may take your leave." Watching her as she went he mused upon her progress. She was still a bit of a wild card. In spite of her confidence, he rather doubted she understood women as well as she thought. *Gentler sex my ass! Give them an inch and they'll take your arm off.*

CHAPTER 8
DELIA

The girl (some would say 'the woman' as she was around seventeen) wasn't happy. Master Timon had brought her to the Temple of Delwyn in Port Weston, despite her objections, and they were now surveying the inner courtyard. It was pleasant enough to look at of course, but that really wasn't the problem. She looked at her companion and inwardly seethed. She knew he believed this was for her own good, deep down in his 'oh-so-kind' heart, but she understood his true motivations better than that. *He's grown tired of me.* That thought alone made her frustration flare again; partly she blamed him, partly herself for being weak. *I should have left him before now, rather than let him dump me here, like some unwanted sack of potatoes.*

"Well?" Master Timon had never been a man of many words, which had suited her fine; it wasn't his words she'd been interested in.

"Oh, it's *lovely*! I simply adore it. I can't wait to meet the other ladies. I'm sure they're all quite charming," her voice dripped sarcasm. She turned her face up to him, complete with an angelic smile.

"Damn it, be serious! This is for your own good. Whether you realize it or not, you need more than I can give. Goddess willing, you'll find it here," his eyes were full of compassion as he spoke. It made her want to slap him.

Instead, she hit him where it would hurt most, "I'm sure the holy brothers here will be able to give me what I require." She had the tip of her index finger between her lips, as though musing over the possibilities.

He had played enough of her games to be familiar with this one, he had no intention of taking the bait, "I'll be back to check on you next spring." He didn't bother asking her to be good; it would just give her another hook for her barbed comments. Turning away, he headed toward the outer gate.

She stood for a moment, unmoving, watching his back as he walked away from her. A sudden gust of wind toyed with her hair and sent the leaves in the yard flying up. A hard knot, formed in her throat. *He's leaving me. Why does everyone leave?* She could feel the tears welling, but she didn't care. The farther he walked the more alone and empty she felt, until at last she couldn't stand it.

"Stop!" A ragged cry tore loose from her throat. Loud and harsh, it was a cry full of tears and pain; her composure was gone, leaving nothing but raw emotion. The ranger turned around, and the force of her body rocked him back on his heels as she flung her arms around him. He straightened and held her gently, while she clung to him, sobbing into his chest.

They stood that way for several minutes, until her breathing eased. At last he slowly disengaged from her, avoiding looking at her too closely. He feared that one look from those liquid green eyes would unman him. She searched his face, wanting one more kiss, but she knew he would not relent.

As the ranger walked out, he passed Islana. She had seen more of the scene than she felt comfortable with, but she hadn't been attempting to eavesdrop. The man's face looked like it had been carved from stone. He said something softly as he walked by, "Take care of her for me." Then he was gone.

She couldn't help but be moved by what she had witnessed. It reminded her of her time with Franz, and that brought with it a lot of emotions she didn't want to face. She smoothed her skirts and cleared her mind; it wouldn't do to greet their new guest with more tears. She had deliberately changed into the simple wool dress she wore on days that she didn't have training, which were few enough. Her instincts told her that armor or leathers might convey the wrong message.

A quick look into the courtyard showed her that the younger woman had gotten her tears under control. *Good, I don't want to embarrass her.* Excessive cheerfulness would probably be offensive, so she chose a simple greeting.

"Hello, my name is Islana. I've been sent to show you your room and give you a small tour if you aren't too tired. If so, we can save that for tomorrow." She kept her expression neutral and her tone friendly. *Sir Brevis wouldn't even recognize me, acting like this.* She rarely bothered to practice gentle social graces around the training grounds. *Shows how much he really knows about women.*

She took a moment to study the woman in front of her, giving her time to compose herself if she needed it. Delia had a striking appearance, with long auburn hair, some of it flowing freely, while the rest was kept in two long braids. The result was functional, yet entirely feminine. She wore soft leathers and carried a long bow stave, currently unstrung. Her complexion was pale, her face round, almost heart shaped, framing two green eyes.

She's beautiful! thought Islana. *I wonder what she'd look like in a gown?*

Delia smiled and broke the silence, "I'm sorry, it's been a long trip, but I'd be very glad of a tour." She was still a bit red around the eyes, but there was no hint in her voice that she'd just been crying. Islana couldn't help but respect the strength that showed.

They walked partway around the temple grounds, talking as they went, but in the end, they cut the tour short. Delia was more tired than she had thought. She bade Islana good night before examining her room. Small and functional, it appeared less comfortable than a woodland bower. The bed was softer than she expected however, and soon enough she was drifting off, images from the past hour passing through her mind. *Islana seemed nice enough, usually women that good looking act like they've got a stick up their arse.* She was sure it was just a matter of time, though. Life had taught her that women rarely liked her for long.

Delia rose with the dawn, and after dressing, she began searching for the dining hall. The day before had left her hungry, for both food and conversation. The first person she ran into was an elderly woman, who showed entirely too much interest in helping her find her destination. After a long and *slow* walk, she finally reached the dining hall. With some relief, she spotted Islana already sitting at a table. Excusing herself, she quickly got some breakfast and made her way over.

The food that morning was sausages and hard rolls. *Not bad,* she thought to herself. She smiled at Islana and began eating in earnest. While she ate, Islana began pointing out various people of interest in the hall, naming them and giving her a description of each person's role and how they fit in at the temple. Most of it was quite tedious. She noticed Islana's eyes lingering on a young man dressed in a simple robe, but she neglected to name him. Delia was nothing if not perceptive.

"Who's that?" Simple questions worked best she had found.

"Who's who?" asked Islana, feigning ignorance.

"That young fellow over there; you haven't mentioned him but you keep looking over that way." She grinned at Islana.

"Oh! That's Thomas, he's just one of the novitiates, young priests in training. No one special, I'm sure you'll meet him in due course," Islana kept her tone neutral.

"He's cute." Delia chewed on her roll, leaning back in her chair casually.

"I wouldn't go that far. He's a bit plain, but I suppose everyone has their own opinion. He's a bit dense when it comes to women anyway." Islana reached for another sausage, then frowned, she'd eaten them already. Her hands seemed awkward without anything to occupy them.

Delia was hot on the scent, her predatory instincts already awake, "I think he's cute, certainly more interesting than most of these old men in here." She gave Islana a wink, thoroughly unsettling her. "A bit dense, huh? I take it you're interested in him?"

"Certainly not," said Islana, a bit too forcefully. The conversation was heading in an uncomfortable direction. "I just meant that, like most of those here he's got more important things to do than seek dalliances."

"Is that what he told you?" Delia was enjoying herself immensely.

"Pardon? Wait, what?" *Did someone tell her about the picnic?*

"Is—that—what—he—told—you?" repeated Delia, pausing dramatically between each word. "You're not fooling anyone, so why not share the story?" She said this last with a conspiratorial whisper.

Flustered, Islana tried to set the record straight, "Look, you've clearly gotten the wrong impression. I've no interest in Thomas or any of the other men here. In any case, he certainly hasn't been discussing his interest in women or lack thereof with me. He's just a friend." She had regained her composure, and she said the last in a cool tone, almost disdainfully.

"Perfect! Then you won't mind if I chat him up a bit?" Her victory was at hand and Delia moved in for the kill.

"Of course not, wait—why? You don't mean..." A woman calmly declaring her intention to pursue a man was beyond Islana's comprehension. It was as though they were speaking different languages.

"Well, yes silly! I just wanted to make sure he wasn't spoken for. I don't want to tread on any toes; you're my first friend here." Her smile was disarming, but Islana could swear it was almost feral.

"This isn't a social club or tavern, Delia. Everyone is here for a purpose, service to our goddess. I don't think it is wise to start out like that. Perhaps after a few months, once you've got your feet under you...," Islana paused; she was at a complete loss for how to continue.

"Isn't that Sir Brevis' wife there—the one you pointed out a minute ago?" asked Delia, putting her new friend off balance.

"Yes, but..."

Delia charged on, "And didn't you say Father Whitmire was married?"

"He's a widower."

"Ok, so he *was* married." This was the most fun Delia had had in ages. "The point I'm getting at, is that there's no reason *not* to look around. Have some fun! Sooner or later you'll find that special someone, but not if you keep your head in the sand."

"That's not on my schedule for the near future," declared Islana. She had gone from bewildered to annoyed. *Have some fun? Sooner or later? What sort of fun is she implying?* "Obviously, we see things a little differently. Why don't you let me show you the rest of the temple? You still haven't seen most of it..."

"One second!" interrupted Delia, rising from her seat. "I'll be right back." Thomas was putting up his dinnerware, and she was moving in that direction. She looked back over her shoulder, "You're sure it's all right?"

Islana shrugged and threw her hands up in a gesture of exasperation. Thomas was looking at her, clearly curious, though he was too far away to hear them. Helplessly, she watched Delia walk over to him. No, walk wasn't quite the right word. *Saunter, or maybe stroll?* She couldn't hear what Delia was saying, but she could see the innocent smile. Then Delia put her hand on Thomas' arm, in an altogether too familiar manner. He was saying something, and then Delia was laughing, casually tossing her hair over her shoulder. A moment later she headed back to their table.

"What was that?" Islana was experiencing several new emotions, all of them irritating. She tried to suppress them.

"Oh! Thomas is going to show me around the library later. I told him you suggested him as my guide, and he seemed quite eager to help. Those brown eyes really are something."

Islana showed her the rest of the temple that morning. Grand Master Brevis had excused her from training so she could help orient Delia, but her initial enthusiasm was gone. Luckily the other girl had stopped asking questions about Thomas, but she still had a sour feeling in her stomach when she thought over that morning in the breakfast hall. Her mind was preoccupied.

"Islana!" Delia was peering at her.

"I'm sorry what?" She realized that Delia had been talking, but she hadn't been paying attention.

"I asked you where the bath was." Delia cocked her head to the side, "You seem distracted, is something wrong?" She had a good idea what might be bothering Islana, but she wasn't about to let on. "No, I'm fine. Sorry I was thinking about an errand I have to do this afternoon." *Brilliant, that'll give me an excuse to get out of this for a while.* "The bath is over here, not far really. I think you'll like it; the temple has the best bath in the city if you ask me. Honestly, it's better even than my father's." *Why did I say that?* Islana made a rule of not discussing her privileged background, for several reasons, one being that wealth was often a barrier to new friendships.

She led her to the open-air bath. Delwyn's temple was unique in that it boasted an outdoor bath built into a small closed courtyard. The walls around it bore no windows, for obvious reasons, and it was too small to contain any trees, but flowers were planted around the edges. Islana was not sure if it was a natural spring, or if some clever architect had designed it, but the water flowing into it was always warm, probably due to the goddess' magic. A small changing room graced the only entrance to it, and the outer door bore a wooden placard which could be changed, depending upon who was inside.

"What's this for?" Delia pointed to the sign.

"It's to avoid accidents." Islana flipped the sign over, on the reverse side it read 'women'. "There are a couple more over there as well, one for privacy, but only the seniors use that, the other is for when they're cleaning."

"Why does this one say 'men' on one side and 'women' on the other?" Delia's face was puzzled.

"So that the men don't walk in when we're bathing! And vice versa I suppose," answered Islana, it seemed perfectly obvious to her.

"That's rather odd. Wouldn't it be a lot more fun with mixed bathing?" suggested Delia.

Islana gaped at her, the very thought made her blush, "No. I don't think it would. Look over here. We shut this door, making sure the sign is up, then you can change in here. Just don't spend more than half an hour or so— sometimes people get impatient." She couldn't wait to get away.

"Aren't you going to bathe as well?" Delia looked a bit disappointed.

"Well, I hadn't planned on it, and I do have some things to take care of."

"Please! I don't want to go in there alone my first time here. What if someone shows up?" She gave Islana her best 'little-girl-lost' look.

In the end Islana relented, she could understand the other woman's nervousness at disrobing in a strange place. After all, the temple was almost eighty percent men, a fact to make any lady careful at a public bath. As they undressed she couldn't help but measure the woman next to her. For a moment, she hoped Delia might have some hidden disfigurement, but she quickly dismissed the idea as uncharitable.

Beneath her rough garments, Delia's body was quite supple. She had a lithe grace and a slender frame, and while not being overly endowed, her proportions were well balanced. She was also surprisingly well muscled. She caught Islana's eye for a second.

"Doesn't look like you have anything to worry about," said Delia, grinning as she slipped into the steaming water. "Oh! This feels good!" Her prior experiences with bathing mostly involved cold streams.

"What do you mean?" Islana tested the water, then eased herself in until it covered her up to her shoulders. She had secretly become quite addicted to bathing since coming to the temple.

"Your breasts! They're very generous. You must garner a lot of looks during training," Delia said this with a mischievous grin, her eyes lit with humor. "Do they interfere when you're sparring?"

"Hah! You should ask Walter about that." Despite her initial annoyance, the warm water improved her mood, and she wound up sharing the story of her sparring match with Walter. That set Delia to laughing, and soon they were chatting like two school girls. *Maybe we could be friends.* Islana decided to reserve judgment for now.

CHAPTER 9
EVENING REFLECTION

An hour later they were dressed, and Islana felt much better for the bath. She had changed her mind about the afternoon, thinking it might not be so bad to spend some more time with Delia. Their plans were interrupted however, when she encountered a messenger in the hall leading to the women's dormitory. "The Grand Master requests your immediate attendance in his study." The guard had a serious bearing.

"Tell him I'll be there as quickly as I can." She said goodbye to Delia and returned to her room to change into her training armor and temple tabard.

Fifteen minutes later she approached Sir Brevis' study. The guard outside wasn't unusual in itself, but the two other men standing across from them were wearing her father's livery. She ignored them and marched into the study without pausing to knock.

Two men were inside the room, one, Sir Brevis looked up at the unannounced entry. If he had been about to say something at the breach of protocol he changed his mind when he saw her face. The second man was her father.

Lord Eisler looked at his daughter and smiled, the same overbearing smile he always wore. His clothes were rich and modestly adorned, his bearing proud, and his eyes carried the same confidence and intelligence that made him a lord to be respected by his peers, and feared by his enemies. "Islana, so good to see you after all this time. We've been quite worried about you."

"Good day, my lord," she responded coldly. Her tone was formal, but her mind was racing.

Her father tilted his head in acknowledgment, "No need to be so formal daughter. Your lady mother sends her greetings. She has been quite beside herself since your hasty departure." He was the very picture of paternal concern. "The Grand Master assures me that you have been well taken care of since your arrival."

"He has been very kind." Islana decided to dispense with the trivialities. "How did you find me, *Father?*" She used the last word with pronounced disdain.

"Sir Brevis was kind enough to send us a letter." He made that statement as though it were a proclamation of victory. "He seems to think you are interested in becoming a temple paladin. I've just been informing him that that won't be possible, given your duty."

Her eyes went to Sir Brevis in shock, but she kept her head, "I have found a different duty, Father. I won't be coming back with you." She had almost said *home*, but that word no longer applied.

Lord Eisler glanced at the senior paladin, "Sir Brevis, might I have a word alone with my daughter?"

Brevis nodded, "Certainly, I'll be outside if you need me." He looked at Islana as he said this, then let himself out.

Lord Eisler turned on his daughter, his face angry, "Do you think to embarrass me in front of him? Your willfulness has gone too far. I expect you to pack up whatever things you've acquired and accompany me when I leave here. Am I understood?"

"You can't bully me any longer. I have decided to devote myself to Delwyn, you have no say in that." She glared at him, a look that might have given a lesser man pause.

"The hell I can't! I've been far too lenient with you before, but that changes right now!" He stepped up to her, and she could see the rage in his face. "Take that ridiculous tabard off and go get your things." He almost snarled the last through clenched teeth.

A calm came over her, "No."

Her face stung, Lord Eisler had slapped her, hard, something he had never done before. "Perhaps you didn't hear me, Father, hasn't anyone told you 'no' before?" Her cheek was red, but she didn't waver.

"Impudent bitch!" His hand rose again, but this time she caught it with her own.

"I allowed you the first strike, out of filial duty," she growled. "I wouldn't test my patience further, if I were you, *Father.*" Her anger filled the room like a blaze.

From outside the room the guards could hear a loud crash, followed by a sound reminiscent of splintering wood. Lord Eisler's guard started to move. "Stop!" Brevis had a commanding voice. "Unless you want to create a diplomatic fiasco, I suggest everyone stay where they are." He looked at the temple guards, "No one is to enter until I come out." So saying, he opened the door and stepped in.

The scene that greeted him inside was like something from a tavern brawl. Lord Eisler stood behind the desk holding a broken chair up in a manner much like a lion tamer. Across from him Islana held what appeared to be a leg from the aforementioned chair. She wielded it much like a club, and her next strike would probably have crushed his skull, if he hadn't warded it with the splintered furniture. *I knew this would happen.* Sir Brevis waded into the room, stepping over a shattered end-table.

Islana spotted him and howled, "No! I am *not* leaving with that pig!"

He barely ducked a wild swing, and got his arms around her. Lord Eisler apparently mistook his intentions, thinking the paladin had come to subdue her. Dropping the chair, he moved to grab her legs. Islana planted both heels in his chest, sending him flying over the desk to land in a crumpled heap.

"Islana! Stop!" shouted Brevis. "You're not going anywhere!" He held onto her though she twisted like a wildcat. Finally, she relaxed. It helped that her father had still not managed to recover from his fall.

Sometime later, they left the room. Lord Eisler looked a bit mussed, but appeared mostly unharmed, except for a minor scalp wound. The rest of his bruises were thankfully hidden, except for the injuries to his dignity. Islana had already been escorted to her room.

Standing at the outer gate Grom was on duty. He held the heavy door as Sir Brevis escorted the nobleman out.

"I won't forget this, Brevis." Even battered, the nobleman managed to threaten; it seemed to be a habit.

"Nor will my office. I'll expect payment for the damages," countered the knight. The Grand Master was not a man to be easily cowed.

Lord Eisler's face grew red, "You!" He seemed at a loss for words. "Fine! Here, take this! Enjoy your whore." He threw a large pouch at the ground, where it exploded, spraying gold coins across the cobblestones. He didn't look back as he marched out, but his guards looked almost embarrassed as they followed.

Once the door was shut, Grom began chuckling, "He should'a been born a dwarf! His mother would ha' left him out for the trogs!" Seeing the look on the Grand Master's face, he decided maybe it wasn't the time for humor, "I'll jus' help ye gather up yer money, perhaps."

Sir Brevis stared at the closed door for a long minute. The angry nobleman's last remarks had finally sparked his temper. *Enjoy your whore.* The words played back in his head. Lord Eisler had come dangerously close to being gutted without ever knowing it. *Fool! Blessed with a daughter like that and you throw your wealth away.* By wealth he wasn't referring to the coins.

Thomas was waiting outside the library when Delia appeared, clad in a soft linen robe. She had a subtle glow about her, and her hair was loose, flowing in gentle waves over her shoulders and down her back. She had spent considerable time combing and brushing it after her bath, not that he would have known that.

Delia smiled delicately at him, "I hope you haven't been waiting long."

"Oh no! Not long," said Thomas immediately. He had actually been inside for an hour already working on an essay for his philosophy class. He had gotten so wrapped up in it that he had nearly lost track of the time. An awkward pause sent him searching for words, "So—do you like books?"

"Not especially," she replied, "but after meeting Islana I thought perhaps I should broaden my horizons." She draped her hand across his arm, "Will you show me inside?" Though she had little experience of courtly graces, she knew quite well how to make a man feel like a gentleman. *Or a beast,* she thought to herself.

Thomas felt clumsy walking her in that way, but he could think of no way to politely extricate himself. The desk clerk raised an eyebrow when he saw him walk in with a beautiful woman adorning his arm, but said nothing. He took her on a quick tour and even showed her the stacks. He was a frequent visitor there, not to mention his time serving as a library assistant. "Is there any particular subject that interests you?"

She considered her reply briefly. Sexual innuendo would be unlikely to carry well at this point, so she kept it simple, "Do they have bestiaries?" Animals she knew, besides it would be interesting to see what men who spent their time buried in parchment and vellum thought about the creatures of the wild. *Probably full of pompous half-truths and fairy tales.*

A short search brought them to a long dusty shelf near the back of the library. *Good choice,* she thought with a smile, *but I'm not yet to that point in the game.* She picked out an impressive volume with an embossed cover. "Will you read it to me?"

That brought him up short, "Can't you read?" He felt like an ass as soon as the question left his lips.

"Some, but not very well," she answered honestly. In point of fact, her reading skills were rather rudimentary. Master Timon had spent some time trying to educate her in this regard, but she had managed to distract him quite thoroughly on most occasions.

"Well no reason not to work on that," said Thomas, leading her over to one of the many reading tables.

They spent the next couple of hours leaning over the book together. Rather than read it to her, he had her practice her own skills, coaching her when the words were too obscure. He didn't seem to notice how close their chairs were.

"We'll have to stop here," he told her at last when he heard the evening bell ring. "The library is about to close."

"Oh no! We can't!" she protested. "This is the first time I've been able to focus like this. Can't we take the book with us?" She looked at him from under long lashes.

Had her eyes always been that green?

"The rules forbid removing books from the library...," Thomas informed her. She frowned as he said this, so he hurried to add, "...but I do have a few primers in my room. You can borrow one of those if you wish."

That earned him a smile. She followed him to the men's dormitory, but she had no intention of borrowing a book.

Once they got to his room he stopped, "Wait here, I'll get one for you."

"Thomas," she said his name with some emphasis, "I don't think I can study it alone. Won't you please help me? It wouldn't hurt for me to come in for a few minutes, would it?" Her face was a combination of plaintive and honest.

His expression was concerned, "If someone saw you entering my room, there'd be all sorts of rumors." He couldn't stand the thought of ruining her reputation. She was far too nice to be the topic of gossip.

"There's no one about right now," she glanced back down the hall as she said this. "I'll make sure no one sees me leaving. You're so gallant to think of a lady's reputation." She opened the door and stepped inside before he could think up any further objections.

He quickly followed, shutting the door. Immediately, he felt that he'd made a mistake letting her in. The room was small, and the only proper furniture was the bed. He started to say as much, but she'd already sat down upon it.

"This is fine; it's actually more comfortable than those chairs in the library anyway." She gave him an innocent look.

There's a girl, on my bed. The room already smelled different, some flowery scent hung in the air. Putting those thoughts aside, he went to his writing table and got his primer on logic and philosophy. Then he paused, unsure where to sit.

"Don't be so stuffy!" She patted the bed next to her, "Here, I won't bite." *Not yet anyway.*

He sat down, already cursing himself mentally, *I'm so wicked to be thinking thoughts like this, she's perfectly innocent.* The bed sank a bit under his weight, drawing them together. He should have moved further apart, but he didn't.

She could see the battle occurring in his mind, but she had no doubt of the outcome. *Just a bit longer, then I'll set the hook.* "So, what's this book about?"

That got him into more familiar territory, and he began to describe the subject in detail. At first, she was bored almost to tears, but his enthusiasm was infectious. Eventually she convinced him to let her read his essay. That turned out to be difficult, and he had to help her with quite a few of the terms. Before long he realized she was very close, too close probably, if anyone were to see them. At some point, she had leaned in against his chest, while his left arm had wound up behind her, the book was resting in his lap. He could feel her warmth radiating through his clothing, but he pushed the thought aside.

It had gotten quite late, and Delia had stopped reading. Moving slightly, he could tell she was asleep. *Now what do I do?* He was pretty sure this was somehow going to turn out badly. Nevertheless, it felt really nice having her there. Her head was nestled against his chest and her hair had a bewitching scent. Without thinking, he leaned over and inhaled deeply. Softly, he lifted her wrist off the book in his lap and set the heavy tome on the floor. Wait. Where had her hand gone? Silly question, he could feel it resting in his lap, ever so close to... *Stop! Stop right there.* He didn't want to think about it.

Fifteen minutes later his back was starting to ache terribly. He was leaning towards her and forward slightly, to support her weight, and the odd position was beginning to leave its toll on him. As much as he hated it, he slowly eased up from the bed, helping her to lie over on her side. She promptly curled up like a cat, fast asleep.

Half an hour after that he was propped uncomfortably against the wall, and his neck was getting sore. Looking over, he realized she was staring at him, her green eyes catlike in the dim lighting. "Don't be stupid Thomas; it's your bed, just lie down up here." Her voice was soft, almost soothing.

"I'm ok, unless you mean you're leaving," he answered, hiding his disappointment as best he could. He probably couldn't sleep on the floor, but having a girl in his bed was such an exotic experience he was willing to lose a night's sleep just watching her breathe.

"No, I'm not going anywhere at this hour, just get in," she told him. "I'm not going to tell anyone. Besides, you've been a perfect gentleman, I'm sure I have nothing to fear." *Too much of a gentleman if you ask me, he's a harder nut to crack than even Timon was.*

Thomas stood up, uncertain, the room was cold, and he was almost shivering. Finally, he made up his mind and started to climb into the bed, but Delia stopped him, "Wait. Take those off. You don't sleep in all those clothes do you?" Her voice was full of amusement.

If the room had suddenly caught fire, he would have been less surprised than that statement made him. *No, I usually sleep naked!* He was pretty sure that wasn't what she intended. *Ok I'll leave the undertunic on.* He slipped his robe and boots off, then his belt and outer tunic. His heart was pounding as he climbed past her to lie near the wall.

Delia slipped the covers over both of them and promptly eased against him, her warm back against his stomach. Thomas was careful not to move. "Here." She reached around and pulled his arm over her, letting it drape across her mid-section. *Do I have to do everything?* she thought silently.

Then again, it was rather exciting to slowly insinuate her way into his arms. If she hadn't been sure before, she was certain now. *He's a virgin... how delicious.* "Just pretend I'm your sister, and it won't bother you so much," she added.

Thomas was fairly sure that if he had had a sister he wouldn't be thinking the thoughts he was at the moment. Nor would he have an erection. He listened to her breathing for a long time, until at last it seemed she had fallen asleep. Finally, he relaxed himself, and without realizing it, drifted into slumber.

Delia crept quietly out of the bed, listening to his light snores for any sign he might wake up. Shimmying, she snaked out of the dress Islana had lent her, pausing for a moment to enjoy the cool air on her skin. Naked, she slipped back under the covers and rolled up against him. He was on his back now and sleeping soundly. Sliding her leg up and over his, she could feel it now, warm against her thigh. *Mmmhhh!* She was trembling with excitement. *I might have to give more thought to virgins in the future.*

She pulled his hand over and placed it on her breast, then she reached down, searching for his manhood. Pulling his tunic up she began to softly fondle him, watching his face. She knew he would wake soon, but by then it would be far too late. *My Thomas! You really are an exceptional man.* His member was swelling rapidly, and its growth was quite prodigious. *Poor Islana, she has no idea what she's missing.* He began to writhe in his sleep, and his breathing quickened.

Thomas' eyes flicked open. Delia's face was inches away, he could feel her soft flesh under his hand, and the sensations coming from his groin were indescribable. Groaning, he moved closer, and her open lips met his. *Surely this isn't happening,* he thought. Her hand was stroking him, guiding his turgid member closer to something warm. She parted her legs, as he rolled atop her, preparing to receive him.

"That's it Thomas! Give me what I want," her voice was crooning in his ear, while her hands gripped his buttocks, encouraging him to seek his pleasure. Something about her tone made him pause, hovering above her. She urged him on, "No, don't tease me! I need it!" She lifted her hips upward.

Thomas was panting, his body quivering, but still, he didn't move.

"She currently sees men and her dealings with them in a very 'transactional' manner," Timon had said. Why was he thinking about that now! Opening his eyes, he could see her beneath him, and there was no doubt in her hungry gaze as to what he should be doing.

"Thomas, please... I need *that* now," she said, staring at the product of his lust.

"If things continue as they have, she'll be nothing more than amoral, devoid of human empathy," Master Timon's words came back to him, even though his body was screaming at him to ignore them.

Finding his determination, he shook his head, "I can't do this to you Delia."

His expression had softened, but she was having none of it. She began reaching, trying to get hold of him. *There's more than one way to skin a cat.* Turning he fought to keep his staff from her grasp. Grabbing her hands, he pinned her to the bed.

"Oh, you like games, eh?" She gave him a wicked look. Lifting her legs, she scissored them around his waist, trying to get some leverage.

"No, Delia. I'm not going to do this. You deserve better," he told her firmly.

She switched tactics and used one leg to push off against the wall. Everything twisted for a moment as they fell to the floor with a thump. Delia knew this wasn't going to work, but she was beyond reason now. She wrestled with him, as if to seek by force what he refused to give. Minutes went by as they struggled on the cold floor, grappling.

"Give me that!" she snarled, trying to reach her goal. Her lithe body was strong beyond belief, and she finally managed to get him on his back, but before she could position herself he had brought his legs up, blocking her way.

Exasperated and panting she swore, "Godsdamnitt! Why won't you fuck me!?" Both their bodies were slick with sweat, which made the cold air doubly uncomfortable.

Something about it all struck Thomas funny, and he began to chuckle. At first it was a semi-hysterical giggle, but it grew into a full bellied laugh quickly. She looked at his face, furious, and then it struck her as well. She didn't give up her grapple, but within moments they were both laughing as they fought on the floor. Finally, the laughter robbed them both of their strength, and they lay entangled like a human pretzel, giggling on the floor like two mad children.

Minutes passed and they laughed themselves out. They had straightened their bodies out a bit, but she still lay curled against him, refusing to let go. Her face was invisible, hidden by her hair and pressed against his chest. He felt her shoulders jerking slightly, and he thought at first she might be laughing again—until her soft sobs became audible. She cried for a long time, and Thomas held her, stroking her hair, as if to sooth a child.

Dawn broke in through the window, stabbing at Thomas' eyes. He was back in bed, clothed now, with Delia curled beside him, also clothed. After their struggle, they had come to some sort of truce, although what it all meant was quite impossible for him to know. Rising from the bed, she gave him a sheepish grin, her hair was tangled and wild.

Not knowing what to say, he glanced at the sun coming through the window.

"I'd better be going, I'm starving, I feel like I've run a mile," said Delia, giving him a strange half-smile. "Check the hall before I step out, or you'll wish you really had done what they'll be saying, if they see me."

He looked out and then nodded to her. Before she left, she grabbed him again, hugging him tightly. "We're still friends, so don't start acting all weird on me."

For some reason that made him think of Islana, although he couldn't immediately see the connection. She let go suddenly, and quick as a flash she was gone. She failed to notice a pair of eyes watching her from the dark end of the corridor.

CHAPTER 10
DRUMANESS

Islana was humming softly to herself while brushing out her long dark hair. A look in the mirror showed a confident young woman staring back at her. In the days since her father's 'visit' she had developed a new sense of purpose. It was as though the experience had solidified something inside her, giving her new resolve. She wasn't overly irritated by Delia's new found closeness to Thomas either, although it still bothered her a little when she saw the girl sitting next to him on a bench, usually with a book in hand.

She had seen them on several occasions, either reading or walking together. They talked amiably, but there was nothing hinting at anything more. Still, she was suspicious. Before this she had never known Thomas to show such interest in anyone, man or woman. *Not that it matters. What do I care what they may or may not be doing?* she cut that thought off abruptly. She knew Thomas well enough to know he wasn't so casual in his relations. She also knew, deep down, that it did matter to her, whether she could admit it or not.

Another summons, this time to the abbot's office, interrupted her thoughts. Dressing in her armor and uniform she wasted no time getting there. She found

Grand Master Brevis waiting within when she arrived, talking amiably with the abbot. He stood and motioned her over, "Islana! Come here, I have something important for you. Did you see Brother Thomas on you way over here?"

"No I didn't, should I have?"

"Doesn't matter, you can relay the gist of this when you see him, but be sure to send him along anyway, he'll need to get his orders directly from Father Whitmire regardless." He quickly filled her in, they were being sent to carry papers to the temple of Kaelan, located in Drumaness. A small trade agreement had been worked out, regarding mead shipments. The only matter remaining to be resolved was the actual delivery of the signed documents. They were to leave at dawn in two days.

Islana waited until he had finished, "One question, sir."

"Go ahead." Sir Brevis always worried when she started a question so formally.

"What exactly is my purpose here? It sounds as though you simply need Thomas, pardon, *Brother* Thomas to deliver the documents and finalize the agreement. What is my part in this?"

The older paladin sighed with relief, as questions went that one was fairly mundane, "It should be readily apparent. You are to provide protection and support, as a defender of the faith."

Islana frowned, "But I'm just a trainee."

"Not any longer, Father Whitmire has agreed you are ready to take your vow. You're to prepare for your vigil tonight." The vigil was a twelve hour fast, from dusk till dawn while she prayed to the goddess for guidance before giving her oath and receiving her vows.

Islana was taken by surprise, she hadn't expected this yet. At best, she had thought it would be at least another year. Unable to figure out a proper response, she thanked them and made her way out.

Once she had left, Whitmire looked at the paladin commander, "You're quite sure about this?"

Brevis nodded, "She's a bit rough, but she shows more promise than I've seen in a decade. She won't gain any more from training exercises. She needs experience." For a moment, he looked old, "I just hope that she grows to meet that potential, rather than die despite it, but that matter is in the goddess' hands."

Islana was walking rapidly, lost in thought. She had to tell *someone*. Then she remembered, she was supposed to look for Thomas. *Surely he'll be happy for me.* In fact, she was rather scared, the responsibility of a paladin's duties seemed too large for her. *Maybe Thomas will have good advice, he's usually got something wise to say.* Abruptly she remembered Grom, Thomas still spent some afternoons helping him at the smithy.

She reached the forge a short time later, but Thomas was nowhere to be seen. Grom looked over, his question unspoken but easily discerned. "Sorry, I'm looking for Thomas," she told him. "Have you seen him lately?"

"Nah, not lately. Why would ye be lookin' fer him?" Something about his eyes hinted at concern.

She wasn't quite ready to reveal her news yet, not until she had shared it with Thomas at least, so she made a feeble attempt at dissembling, "Nothing important, I just haven't talked to him much lately and he's been a bit distracted. I thought he might be able to help me with a question I had." She paused, then decided her remark sounded a bit too much like that of a girl seeking attention. "...about the faith. Theology, nothing personal," she amended. *That didn't help.*

The dwarf sighed, setting down his hammer. *She's settin' her cap for someone who'll only bring her sorrow,* he thought to himself. It was not in Grom's nature to interfere, but he'd grown fond of her over the past year. She had more fire in her than most and she had never shown herself to be mean spirited. Violent on occasion, but not without cause. "Maybe ye might rethink yer plan."

"What?" It was entirely out of character for Grom to offer advice. "What plan?"

"Now lass, I know ye've set yer bonnet on that young priest, but I don' think any good will come of it." Now that he'd opened his mouth there was no getting around the subject.

That put her on the defensive, "I think you're making a mistake, I haven't, 'set my bonnet' on anyone. What does that mean anyway? I'm not some schoolgirl. I have no intention of chasing men at present anyway."

"Now don't be like that. Ye're not foolin' me none. I just think ye'd be better served lookin' elsewhere." Grom glanced at the bar on his anvil, the metal had cooled, and would need to be reheated, but there was no help for that now.

Islana stared hard at the smith, her intuition was clamoring for her attention. "What are you trying to tell me Grom? You sound as if you know something."

"Nah, don't be after me to talk about other people's trysts. Its none of me affair, I just wanted to save ye some tears," as soon as the words left his lips he knew he had slipped.

Trysts? Trysts! "What are you not telling me? Have you seen Thomas with someone?" The conversation went in circles for a while, with Grom trying to turn her questions aside, but he was no match for her verbal sparring. Defeated at last, he gave up the battle.

"Fine! Fine! I saw that new girl leavin' his room, at a rather unusual hour. An' before that they was a wailin' and carryin' on as if there was a war goin' on in there. An' not the sort of war where folks are dyin' neither. More the sort of war that comes after the war, where everyone's makin' up and decidin' who's paying the reparations. Na' wait, that doesn't make sense either. Lemme start over, ok so let's say ye've got a cat, and it's that time, and there's a tom roamin' around, so she starts yowlin' and makin' an awful racket. Now if ye…"

Islana was turning several shades of red, "Enough! I get the idea." She had never heard the dwarf utter so many words at one time, and he showed no sign of finishing without help. "Thank you, Grom. You've been most illuminating. Don't worry yourself though, I'm not interested in Thomas in the least, nor do I care what he does in his room when the lights are out."

"Jus' don't kill him and we'll all do fine," replied the dwarf, but she was already walking away.

"Tom roamin' around, now that was funny," he began mumbling to himself, "cuz tom is short fer Thomas. Ah me, he's going ta' be right mad when he finds out I told her that."

In the end, she didn't find Thomas, he happened across a messenger and was in the abbot's office even as she was talking to Grom. She didn't look for him the next day either, it had taken the better part of the night to clear her mind. The ceremony had filled her with a calm energy and left her renewed in spirit and purpose. It also left her exhausted. She spent the entire morning sleeping afterward.

As a result, she didn't see Thomas until the morning they were to set out for Drumaness. He was standing at the front gate waiting when she arrived, a small pack on his back and a scimitar belted at his side. The sword didn't surprise her; the scimitar was the favored weapon of Delwyn and since his ordination a few months prior he had taken to training with it more seriously. She had been his sparring partner on more than one occasion.

Looking at him now, she felt sad, and his friendly smile and happiness to see her did nothing to help either. He spent the better part of their first hour on the road congratulating her and making small talk. He seemed excited by their mission, the first either of them had received. She tried to keep up with the banter and small talk, but it got increasingly difficult. Every time he smiled at her she saw him in her mind, lying atop Delia, grunting and sweating like a beast in rut.

"Who would have thought we'd be sent out together?! Remember when we first met? A couple of years ago—you were magnificent saving that child, and when you punched Sir Brevis! Ha! I thought the world was going to end, I've never seen anyone do that before, or since. Back then—I couldn't have imagined you here today! Look at you!" Normally Thomas was perceptive enough to catch onto her moods, but today he seemed oblivious.

In fact, he had noticed her somber mood. It was hard not to, given her monosyllabic responses, but he didn't know what else to do. So he kept on, hoping to lift her spirits. "I might be wrong, but I'll bet you're the first female paladin to take the vows in the last five years. Certainly you're the most beautiful..." It wasn't like him to compliment her looks, but he was desperate to cheer her up.

"Thomas...," she said quietly. He paused and looked at her. "...If you're looking for a woman to please, I'm sure there will be plenty in Drumaness. I for one am not interested in your flattery or praise." She kept her tone level, but the words hit him like cold water.

A strange looked crossed his face, and he started to open his mouth, but then thought better of it.

They resumed walking, the chilly silence casting a pall over the road ahead. After a few miles, he spoke up, "I was just happy for you." She could hear his sincerity, but it only made her madder. She bit back an angry response, although she did growl audibly.

A few minutes later he broke the silence again, "What did you mean, 'a woman to please'? Do you think I'm that shallow?" His own bitterness was showing now.

Something tore loose within her, "No Thomas, I know you aren't shallow. In fact, you're very nice, so nice the whole world can't help but notice! You think I don't know how 'deep' you are? Trust me, I know! You're probably the nicest man I've ever met. You're so considerate, so kind, I wonder that you ever have time to please yourself! In point of fact, I was thinking of *you* when I said that; it seems to me you deserve some kindness yourself. So when I said, 'a woman to please' what I really meant, was that you should find some whore to spend yourself on! I just don't want to be that whore, so don't waste your time telling *me* that I'm beautiful!" She was yelling now, and every word was the truth, even though sarcasm made them into weapons. Large tears began to roll down her cheeks as she finished. She turned her back to hide them.

His footsteps crunched in the gravel as he walked up behind her. *He just doesn't know when to give up does he?* His hand was almost to her shoulder when she warned him, "Don't." There was a lethal tone in her voice. "Leave me alone Thomas, it's better that way."

The rest of the day was spent in silence, and even when setting up camp they managed without saying a word. A small fire failed to warm them as they ate a cold dinner; neither of them had felt like cooking. That night Thomas lay watching the stars, sleep beyond his reach, much as they were. Instead, he mulled her words over in his mind, casting about for reasons, but logic was no help.

The dawn found them exhausted, but they rose and trudged onward. The land was beginning to roll as they got into the foothills; grassy knolls and rocky outcroppings became increasingly common. Near midday they came to the top of a rise in the road, the view ahead stretching for miles. Staring at the vista before them, Islana came to a decision. "Thomas." She saw him stop, waiting to see what she would say. "I am sorry for what I said yesterday, you didn't deserve that."

"Well I'm sure if you'll just tell me what has you so mad at me, we can figure something out. You're my best friend, Islana. Just trust me with whatever it is that's bothering you." The sunlight had given his brown hair golden highlights.

Best friend. Those words stood out in her mind. *That's the problem, but you can't see that.* She walked closer, until they were standing just a foot apart, "Have you ever thought, that maybe, just maybe, I didn't want to be *friends?*" Islana was tall for a woman, her eyes almost level with his own; he could see the sadness in them.

His eyes widened, "Huh?" *Didn't want to be friends, what?* "I'm confused."

Islana gave up, "You're such an idiot." She said that almost tenderly. Leaning forward, she hugged him, something she had never done before.

He held onto her, "Why don't you want to be friends?"

"Just shut up. We are friends. See, I'm hugging you." Islana had made peace with herself. Her anger was gone, leaving her just a bit sad. It felt good holding him, but he was not hers. She pushed him away.

They began walking again, trying to reach the town before the afternoon was gone. The mood had lightened considerably, and they talked more easily now, but Thomas pondered their situation. He just couldn't understand women. He was beginning to wonder if he *wanted* to understand them. *One tries to make my wildest fantasies come true, but I can't do a thing because it'll hurt her more. The other is beautiful and completely unapproachable. Says she doesn't want to be friends, but we're friends anyway. I honestly think they're trying to drive me mad.*

They arrived in Drumaness an hour later. The temple of Kaelan was the most prominent building in town, so it wasn't hard to find. The god they worshiped there was fond of wine and drink, so fond in fact, that the priests wore stoles emblazoned with an ale mug. The town itself was known for its fine ales and produced several excellent meads.

The man at the main entrance to the temple looked a bit rough, but he was friendly enough and quickly ushered them inside. They were asked to wait in the main sanctuary, the heart of the temple proper, if it could be called that. Kaelan's primary area of worship was essentially an ale hall. The entire floor was dominated with feast tables and against the far wall was a bar. The whole affair would have looked normal, in a tavern, if it were very large, except for the large golden chalice displayed behind said bar. The term 'chalice' wasn't quite right either, since it had the form of a very large beer stein. It was encrusted with jewels and probably worth a fortune, not that anyone could sell such a thing; it was their holiest relic.

A few of the more devout worshipers were sitting at the bar venerating their god. At any other place, they would have been considered drunks, starting an early binge. Evening had not yet come, so the majority of the congregation were still out working in the fields. Thomas and Islana took a seat at the bar and tried to get their bearings.

Thomas eyed the nearest 'patron' and decided to take a chance, "Excuse me, I'm looking for the high priest, would you happen to know if he's here today?"

The man belched and leaned over, "Aye laddie, he's about here somewhere. Sure an' he'll be back soon, lest our mugs run dry!" Thomas took that to mean that the chief priest would be back soon.

A moment later a man entered the bar from the back, carrying a large cask. He wore a brown robe and the customary red stole. His beard was red as well, but its shade clashed with that of his raiment. Seeing them at the bar he set his cask down and came over.

"Fit like?" The priest's accent was unintelligible, at least to Thomas' ear.

"I'm sorry, what?"

"He's asking if you're well, it's a common greeting here," explained Islana, grinning.

Grateful, Thomas answered, "I'm fine thanks. Is Father Ewen Macaulay here?"

"Sorry lad, I din' ken ye were from Port Weston. I be Ewen, when the mood suits!" His accent was much less pronounced now that he knew they were from Weston.

He introduced himself, "I'm Brother Thomas, from the temple of Delwyn. I'm here to deliver some documents." He started to draw the papers out, but Ewen waved at him to put them away.

"Nae lad, ye must be puggled from yer journey. Dinnae fash yersel'." Thomas was confused, but again Islana helped him to understand the thick brogue.

"He's telling you to take it easy, you must be tired." Her job translating seemed to be amusing her. With Islana's help they managed to figure out what 'Father' Ewen was saying. After a while it became clear that they were expected to spend the night. The evening's devotions would be starting in a couple of hours so they were led to their rooms and given time to refresh themselves.

Thomas' room was quite sumptuous, at least by the standards he was used to. It was a relief to finally have some privacy. The difficulties of understanding the local dialect had worn on his nerves. Thomas wasn't aware of having fallen asleep until he heard a knock at the door.

Islana was standing there when he opened it, but her appearance had changed dramatically. She wore a long green skirt topped by a white chemise. The sleeves were long and full, gathered at the cuffs, while the neckline was modest. Draped round her shoulders was a long plaid stole and a bright sapphire pendant hung at her neck complimenting her eyes. Her hair was free and loose, except for a small braid on one side.

Thomas' eyes went wide, and his mouth dropped. He stood gaping for a moment, "What happened to you? How? You look like a native of Drumaness."

Islana smirked at him, "May I come in? Or do you plan on leaving a lady standing in the door?" It wasn't really a question since she was already stepping inside. After a moment, she explained her change of appearance, "My father has some business dealings in Drumaness, so—when I was younger, Mother and I would sometimes come with him. She loved it here, so we often spent several weeks at a time. As a result, I made a few friends. These...," she gestured at her garments, "...are from my friend, Nansaidh." She pronounced the name much like 'Nancy' but with a slightly different lilt.

"Now your familiarity with the speech here makes sense," said Thomas. This was a new facet of Islana, one that he'd had no hint of before. "Did she lend you that necklace as well? It's lovely. It perfectly matches your eyes." *Fool! If 'beautiful' upset her what will that remark do?* he silently cursed himself.

Islana's reaction was entirely different however; she smiled and looked away for a moment, rising to look out the window, which hid her slight blush from his view. "No, it was from Mother, she bought it for me on our last trip here together. That's probably why I brought it."

"You've never said much about your parents," it was more a question than a statement.

"No... I haven't." She gave him a serious look before breaking the tension, "Have you ever danced a strathspey?"

"A what?"

She laughed, "A strathspey, one of the country dances they have here. You're going to have to learn, there's a *Feis* tonight."

That required some explanation, but it turned out that they had arrived on the day of a small festival.

Consequently, the temple of Kaelan would be full of people that night. With a bit of cajoling she walked him through the steps of the strathspey, humming a tune to keep time.

After a bit, he started to get over his anxiety at the thought of dancing. "That's not so bad," he commented.

"If you do well at that, maybe I'll try to teach you a reel later, but we'll need live music. I can't hum it," she told him.

"Did you visit the temple before, when you were younger?" Thomas was curious about the change that had come over Islana in Drumaness. In some ways, she almost seemed a completely different person. She'd never been so forthcoming about her past before, either.

Islana feigned shock, "Oh no! Father wouldn't let me anywhere near this place; entirely too much drinking and wild behavior for his daughter to be seen here."

The time was getting late so they went down to the main hall again. It had been transformed from its previous arrangement. Several large trestle tables in the center had been moved back, creating a clear space, which was full of people standing and talking. One corner had a makeshift platform erected, on which stood several musicians idling.

They found a seat just as the music started, and Ewan stopped to talk to them for a time. A bewildering conversation with the priest of Kaelan made a few things clear, with Islana's help of course. One, the Brothers of Kaelan didn't care nearly as much about the written agreement as the temple of Delwyn did. Second, they were expected to drink, dance and enjoy the evening.

Apparently, a long drinking session was the best way to seal any arrangement. Thomas was starting to grasp the true reason the abbot had sent him instead of coming himself; Father Whitmire had sworn off drinking years ago, after finding a certain orphan.

The music had grown louder, forcing them to lean in closely to hear one another. Islana was saying something about ale, but the words were unfamiliar, so she still had to repeat herself before he understood. Drumaness boasted a number of good ales, but they were most famous for their mead, which wasn't produced in many other places. Thomas knew next to nothing about ale, so he took Islana's advice and they both had the sweet mead, which turned out to be an amazingly delicious drink.

After one glass of that Thomas knew it would be a good idea to wait a while before drinking more, but Father Ewan was having none of it. He wouldn't leave them alone until he was sure they'd both had a second glass and were considering a third. Then he wandered off to talk to a few others.

At last the musicians started to play a tune suitable for the strathspey, and Thomas was lured from his perch by a combination of the mead already in him and Islana's coaxing. The alcohol had loosened him up, and after successfully managing the strathspey he felt confident the 'reel' would be easy. They paused for a few more sips of mead, and then he led her back onto the floor.

The 'reel' was quite a bit faster than the dance before and soon Thomas was quite lost. Islana was laughing at his predicament, but neither of them was willing to give up. Thomas improved over the next hour and soon they were swirling and skirling with the others on the floor, caught up in a mad frenzy. During the breaks between dancing, they found themselves very thirsty, which was easily remedied; the mead was flowing freely.

Later, they stumbled out of the crowd, breathless and perspiring; they were utterly exhausted when they dropped into their seats at the large trestle. The drinks and dancing had set their heads spinning and put a flush in their cheeks. Peering at Islana from the corner of his eye, Thomas wondered at his luck, dancing with such a lovely woman. The cacophony was even louder now, so he inclined his head to reach her ear, "We should have done this before!"

"You never asked," she shouted back.

"I've never danced before; you should have told me it was so much fun!" he responded.

"Huh?" she asked.

She couldn't hear him, so rather than shout louder, he leaned in until his lips were close to her ear and repeated himself. It seemed like a good way to talk, so they crowded close together, exchanging words and glances over the music. It also felt quite natural having his arm around her, after they had been dancing so long.

"Why did you ask me to a picnic that time?" They had stopped talking, and he'd been staring deeply into her eyes for a minute or more, when he said this. Thomas was certain that she was the most beautiful thing he'd ever seen.

Her answer was slightly slurred, "I wanted to make you smile." That got him to questioning, in the serious manner that drunks the world over are prone to—until finally she explained, "You were always so serious, so mysterious. You were worrying about other people, but I could tell you were bearing a great weight. Then you smiled at me, that day after I got sent to the Abbot. The world lit up when you smiled, and I thought—if I could just make you smile again, maybe..." Her eyes were huge, liquid pools drawing him into a mystery he could hardly fathom.

The room seemed to be moving under him, an unwelcome distraction. "I think we've had too much to dink, m'dear." He rose to his feet unsteadily, and then proffered his hand, "if the lady wishes, I can eshcort you to your room."

She giggled at his poor articulation as he helped her up. Navigating in eccentric curves and zigzags, they at last made it up the stairs and to their rooms, coming to a halt outside Islana's door. Neither of them had retained much balance, so she leaned back against the wood with her hands folded behind her.

Thomas bid her good night, then looked back. She was still there, with a look that made him sure he had left something undone. Turning, he put his hand on the wooden panel beside her head, "I think I forgot something." His voice was deeper now.

"I think you did...," Islana lifted her chin, looking up at him with challenging eyes.

Lowering his lips to hers, he thought at first to make the kiss simple and straightforward, but that was not to be. Her arm encircled his neck, and he felt her lips parting as the kiss grew deeper. Without conscious thought, his own arms were around her waist, pulling her close.

Islana was swept up in a storm, her passion driving her to abandon. Thomas' lips seemed to be everywhere as he pressed her against the door. She could feel one hand cupping her bottom, kneading and pulling her hips against his, while his mouth had found the side of her neck. Suddenly the door opened behind her, and he was walking her backwards toward the bed. Her body felt as if it were on fire as she pulled him down atop her.

An eternity passed as their long-repressed feelings became manifest through their lips and hands. The alcohol had numbed Islana's senses, but Thomas' hand felt like a living brand as it snaked under her shirt, questing, caressing. *I never imagined he contained so much passion,* she thought, moaning even as he kissed her again. *Was it like this for Delia?* That thought stopped her cold.

"Wait—stop—Thomas!" She pushed him off the bed and sat up, confused and flustered.

"What!?" He was vexed, rubbing a sore spot on his head.

"You need to go, this is wrong." *I will not be a consolation prize.*

"Aghh! You are the most confusing woman alive!" Gaining his feet, he headed for the door, narrowly missing the chair.

I'm not the woman you should be trying to figure out, she thought. Then the tears started and wouldn't stop, not for a long while. She felt as though the world was crumbling around her, and it seemed like hours before she finally fell into a deep and dreamless slumber.

Lying in the hallway, Thomas listened to her sobbing. He hadn't quite managed to make it to his room, instead discovering that the floor seemed much more comfortable. Much later, he woke in the darkened hallway and barely managed to make it outside before he threw up. *Surely I couldn't have had this much in my stomach.*

When he got back to his room he lay on the bed, trying to make the world stop spinning, "This trip to Drumaness has turned into a stunning success." *One woman tries her damndest to force me, the other tempts and rejects me even though I'm willing.* Sleep, when it finally came, was a welcome relief.

CHAPTER 11
A Night Under the Stars

Neither one of them was awake to greet the dawn. It was nearly noon before they met Father Ewan downstairs, and they made a point of not speaking to each other. Their mission had been a success, at least as far as the priest of Kaelan was concerned, so he fed them and sent them on their way in the early afternoon.

It was several hours before Thomas spoke, "About last night..." The sun was close to setting. "I'm sorry, I was drunk and maybe I misread things. I hope you can forgive my actions." His voice was wooden.

"You idiot." *Why does he always blame himself?* she thought.

"Well yeah, that's what I mean, I was an idiot. What I did, that's not the sort of man I'm trying to become. You have every right to be angry, and I'm thankful that you stopped me when you did," he told her somberly.

"Yes, it's a good thing I did. Obviously, if I hadn't, you might have ruined me," her voice was dripping with sarcasm. "Thankful, you're *thankful!* Did it ever occur to you, that perhaps you weren't the *only* one involved? Is it so inconceivable that *I* had something to do with what happened?"

"Well if you weren't being mauled by me, if you were a willing participant, what the hell happened?" His frustration from the night before had returned in full force.

"I came to my senses. I got caught up in the moment, and *we* nearly made a mistake. Our friendship is more important to me than that, just don't try to devalue my part by assuming that you were making all the decisions last night." Surprisingly she felt much calmer now.

Thomas nodded, "You're right. Our friendship is important. Not only that, we both have responsibilities given our new roles at the temple. We are still friends, right?" He waited, not sure what she might say.

"Yes, we're friends, but don't push it, I'm still mad at you." She started walking again, trying to pick out where they would do best to set up camp.

Once again Thomas was confused, "I don't get it, *why* are you mad? Yesterday you tell me you didn't want to be friends, but we are, now you say you want to be friends but you're mad at me."

"You just need to figure out who you *don't* want to be friends with," she replied primly.

"Obviously, that made sense." Thomas was developing the fine art of sarcasm.

"Yes, yes it did," said Islana, and she refused to comment further.

They made camp, but this night they took the extra time to set up a cook-fire and heat their meal. Despite the confusion, they had settled into an uneasy truce. By mutual consent they put their bedrolls on opposite sides of the camp, as far apart as practical.

Islana started awake, a large hand was covering her mouth, forcing her head against the ground. More hands caught her arms and someone was gripping her legs. At least three men held her, trying to lift her. They smelled of smoke and sweat, an acrid stench that filled her nostrils. Panic threatened to overwhelm her but she fought it down, clearing her mind to deal with the present. *Think Islana, think! What do they want?* Sir Brevis had spent considerable time making sure his students knew that every trial began with winning the battle inside yourself. Islana would not fail that task.

They were moving now, carefully working to get her away from the camp as quietly as possible. *They're separating us.* A chill went down her spine, she knew what they wanted. She quickly inventoried her position, *my armor is by the fire, so are the weapons.* They were already fifteen feet or more from there, and steadily getting farther away. *My own weapons are too far, what do they have?*

The men holding her were clad in rough leather, and she thought she could see the hilt of a knife at the belt of the man holding her mid-section. Her assessment didn't get very far; Thomas rushed out of the darkness, charging into them. He came in low, knocking the feet out from under two of them, and everything dissolved into chaos.

Two of her assailants had lost their grip on her legs and arms, they were scuffling on the ground now. The one holding her head jerked her upright, one hand still over her mouth while his other arm sought to pin her hands. She saw a club rising and falling in the shadows as Thomas fought to stand. Once, twice, it struck him in the stomach, then his arm, until finally it found his head. Soundlessly he crumpled to the ground.

She bit down *hard*, ripping a chunk of flesh from her opponent's hand. He screamed and lost his grip, slipping on the dry leaves littering the ground. He never recovered. Twisting to the side, she swept his legs out from under him. He started to rise, but she grabbed his head with one hand and drove her knee into his face.

Teeth cut into her leg through her linen shift as his jaw broke, it should have been painful yet she felt nothing. Reaching down, she drew a short, cruel sword from his waistband. The other two men had not been idle. One was striding toward her, club raised, already laughing at his companion's misfortune. Her eyes flicked to the one behind him, he had a long-knife in hand, preparing to deliver a coup-de-grace to the unconscious priest.

Time slowed as she sped up, the man before her swung with his club. Rather than dodge, she stepped into him, and the cudgel struck poorly, glancing down her shoulder and back. Not pausing, she shoved the overbalanced man, sending him falling sideways. Her next step brought her in range of the man with the blade, and seeing her, he brought his knife up between them. The sword in her hand swept forward, slicing the outer part of his hand away; the return stroke opened his throat. Blood fountained outward, spraying across her in an obscene shower as he fell back, dying.

Turning back, she saw that the man with the club had already risen. She smiled at him, her teeth stained crimson. His wild swing failed to connect, and then she impaled him, driving the sword upward, through his sternum and out his back. Almost gently, she eased him to the ground, sliding the sword from its bloody sheath in his chest.

A sharp pain blossomed in her chest and she looked down, not comprehending the feathered shaft standing out from her breast. The man with the broken jaw stood a few feet away, a crossbow in hand, now empty. She closed quickly, before he could recover, but her sword failed to find purchase as she struck. A long gash opened up along his arm, dark and ugly. Dropping the crossbow, he caught her sword arm before she could finish him.

The struggle that followed was slow and desperate. Unable to keep her balance, she wrestled with him on the ground. At the end, she sat atop him, driving the sword slowly downward with the weight of her body. He was clutching the blade vainly with his hands, the edge cutting through his palms. Hands slick with blood he could no longer maintain his hold on the steel blade as she inexorably pushed downward. She could hear him begging as it slid into him, slipping between his ribs. His final sobbing breaths were cut short when it finally pierced his lungs.

She tried to get up, but something was wrong with her. She couldn't breathe, and her limbs refused to listen to her anymore. Slipping to the side she slid to the ground next to the dying man. Her last thought as darkness closed around her, was to thank the goddess, but she couldn't be sure if she was heard.

Thomas came to slowly. He was lying on the ground in the dark. Dim light from the fire showed him the crumpled forms around him. Sluggishly he tried to rise, but nausea overwhelmed him and he began to retch. Feeling his skull, he found a soft mushy spot, which brought fresh waves of pain. His hand came away slick with what he thought must be blood.

Crawling, he searched among the bodies, until at last he found her. Her nightclothes were soaked with blood, and more was pumping slowly out around the bolt in her chest. "No! No, no, no!" he moaned, as if words could reject the reality in front of him. *She'll die in front of me if I don't do something.* He knew there was little hope, however. *If I draw the bolt, she'll bleed out. If I don't, she'll die just as surely.*

Bowing his head, he began to pray. His skills as a cleric were still small, and his spells were limited to orisons and minor blessings. Focusing his mind, he sought to connect with Delwyn more directly, to go beyond simple clerical spells to divine intervention. *Please, you helped Grom. She's dying.* In the cool darkness, he got no reply, but a gentle warmth filled his mind.

He uttered a short chant, and light began to shine from the symbol he wore around his neck. The carnage around him came to life in bright colors, pale skin and dark red blood. Islana was the only one still breathing, and he could hear a bubbling sound as her chest rose. *It's through her lung.* There were no more choices, it had to come out. He only had one healing spell which should at least stop the bleeding and keep her from dying. *If* she survives having the bolt drawn first…

He cast about for a few minutes until he found the crossbow and a few other bolts scattered where it had been hastily dropped. Examining the points, he was relieved to see they were leaf-heads rather than barbed.

Islana screamed in agony, or would have, but all that came out was a gurgling wheeze. Her eyes locked onto Thomas as he tugged at something terribly painful. She felt a ripping sensation and then it was out. Briefly she saw the red shaft in his hand before he tossed it away. Bright light was pouring from something hanging at his chest and she could see a dark line of blood running from his scalp to his neck. "You need to have that looked at," she tried to say, but her voice wouldn't work; she was drowning.

Thomas looked at her as she lay gaping, struggling to draw breath. *Goddess please!* Uttering the words, he felt her magic flowing through him, passing into Islana's ruined lungs, and then it was gone. Straining, he waited, seconds passing like hours. The horrible gurgling had stopped, but was she breathing, or dead? Then he saw her chest slowly rise, and she began to cough, clearing the blood from her throat.

The entry wound was still there, bloody and raw, but it was no longer seeping, so he cut strips from his tunic to bind it. Her own tunic was soaked in blood, ruined, so he cut it off and wrapped her in the blanket from her bedroll. He dragged his backpack over, searching for water to give her, when he heard new voices.

There are more of them? Quickly slinging his backpack over his shoulder, he leaned down and slipped one arm underneath Islana's shoulders, the other beneath her legs. Adrenaline had given him such strength that she felt light as he stood up again, but he knew it had to be illusion. Studying the foliage at the edge of their camp, he began to work his way in among the trees, leaving the open road behind.

"Over here!" A man's voice, loud in the quiet shadows; Thomas wasn't nearly far enough away yet. "I found Wills, and Dougal, they're dead!" More voices answered, but he couldn't tell how many there were. "Light! There's a light back there!"

Thomas had been using his holy symbol to light the path, hoping to gain enough distance, but it had given them away now. Cursing silently, he whispered a word, and the light vanished. He found himself now in pitch darkness, and behind him the underbrush was rustling as they searched for them. It felt as if he and Islana had been swallowed by a black void, and he had no sense of movement as he walked. Step by step he kept going, branches clutching at their clothes and hair. In front of him he could see a soft light which soon resolved itself. Sarah was beckoning to him, and he passed through an endless empty space, while invisible vines and brush fell away from them.

Eternity swelled and crashed over him in ceaseless waves, sprinkled with stars. The only sensation left was that of his legs moving, driving him onward. Dawn found him standing beside a brook, water rushing by over mossy rocks. A massive tree stood before him, one side rotten, opening into a semicircular area where the heartwood had once been.

Not knowing what else to do, he went in, still carrying Islana, though he knew not if she was still alive. The cool air within seemed welcoming as he lay her down. He gathered moss to fashion a pillow for her head.

At last he could do no more, so he lay down beside her, and sleep came for him like an old friend, stealing his pain away.

CHAPTER 12
CONFESSION

Grom was worried. Six days had passed since Thomas and Islana had left Port Weston. They should have returned sometime in the evening two days ago. Something was wrong. He had made his feelings known to Captain Martin, but the guard officer felt that Grom should leave such concerns for wiser heads to decide.

The dwarf had not wound up at the temple of Delwyn in Port Weston by waiting around for 'wiser' heads to pull themselves out of their respective arses. He needed help however, for he had no skill at tracking. There being no experienced rangers currently at the temple, he thought of Delia. Not only did she have the requisite skills, but from what he had seen and heard previously, he thought she might be willing to help.

As it turned out his intuition was correct. Delia was already missing them both, if for different reasons. What she hadn't known was that they were overdue to return. She agreed to travel with him immediately, indeed she would have set out then, but dusk was upon them already.

The next morning they were ready and already heading out the gate when the captain hailed Grom, "Ho! Grom, a word if you please." The dwarf took a deep breath. He was no longer on parole, but being in the service of the temple guard, his actions were taking him into bad territory. Technically, leaving without permission was desertion of duty. In peaceful times that merited strong disciplinary measures, if it were during a time of war the punishment was death. Not that any of that would have stopped him.

"Yes, ser!" He waited obediently as the captain strode toward him.

"You are on gate duty today if I'm not mistaken." Captain Martin frowned down at him, not failing to notice the travel pack on his back, "Taking a trip, Mister Grom?"

"No ser, I was a wee bit hungry this morning, so I thought I'd bring some extra food to the gate to keep me stomach from growlin'." The dwarf's face was entirely serious.

"I'm afraid you won't be able to perform that duty this morning. I took your concerns to Grand Master Brevis. You are to take the apprentice ranger, Delia and set out in search of Brother Thomas and Islana." The captain glanced at Delia, tipping his cap for a moment. "You would be Miss Delia I presume?"

Delia smiled, "Delighted to make your acquaintance captain."

Martin looked back at Grom, "How fortunate, I see Miss Delia is also equipped with snacks and a bedroll."

"The weather has been so nice I thought I'd eat lunch outside." She was positively beaming at the captain.

"It's six in the morning," replied the guard captain.

Delia winked at him, "I woke early and had breakfast at three. You should try it sometime captain, it's very invigorating. Perhaps we could have breakfast together one morning—say around two a.m. or so?"

Grom intervened, "We'd best get movin', Captain." He nudged Delia and they headed for the gate once more.

They traveled for a day and a half before they saw the vultures. They picked up their pace, as it looked like the area the birds were circling might be on the road a mile or two ahead. When they rounded a bend half a mile further on, their fears were confirmed. The bodies were bloated with gas and gave off an incredible stench. The skin of their faces was so swollen and distorted it was hard to identify them. Islana's armor and weapons lay near the remains of a cold fire.

Delia surprised the dwarf with her lack of squeamishness. Quite the contrary, she quickly began examining the corpses. She rolled each on its the side to check for insects, opened their shirts to see what their skin looked like, and even went so far as to verify their gender. After a few minutes her poking and prodding began to make even the normally stoic dwarf ill.

"They've been dead for four, maybe five days at most," said Delia clinically. "Their limbs are loose, so their death rigors have passed, and the bloating means they've started to putrefy." Delia shook one of the corpses' arms to illustrate her point.

"Ye can stop doin' that, if ye don't mind." Grom was distinctly uncomfortable at the casual way she dealt with the decaying bodies. "Any idea who they were or what might've happened to them?" Left unspoken was the concern that something similar had happened to their friends.

"I can't be absolutely sure, but at a guess, they crept into the camp at night and attacked them. Islana killed these three but was badly wounded. Then she and Thomas escaped into the brush over there...," she pointed at the brush and scrubby trees leading into the hills.

The dwarf gaped at her, "How'd ye get all that from three bodies?" Grom knew of rangers who might be able to read a cold camp that well, but this was more than he expected from the young woman.

Delia pointed at the remains of the campfire, "The ashes are smudged and kicked up, but the fire was never banked, which would indicate it happened at night. Thomas couldn't possibly have fought and killed all these men, so it's likely she did; I've seen her sparring. I almost feel sorry for them."

"But her gear and weapons are still here. Ye're saying she killed 'em barehanded and unarmored?" asked Grom. He was still doubtful, but what she said had made sense so far.

The ranger nodded, "Exactly. All three of them died by that sword," she indicated a shortsword still sticking up from one body. Walking over, she pulled it out and slid it back into the sheath at the man's waist. "See, he died from his own sword. She took it from him and then used it to kill all three; probably he was the last one."

Grom whistled in appreciation, "So then she and Thomas ran?"

She shook her head negatively, "Unlikely. This fellow had his jaw broken, and he was killed with his own sword. She probably took the weapon from him, breaking his jaw in the process, killed those two and then stabbed him after he shot her."

"Shot her?"

"Mm hmm—the crossbow is over there. Very likely, he shot her in the back while she was dispatching his friends, then she came back and finished the job with him."

"Maybe he missed, and she finished him off," suggested Grom, still holding out hope.

"Nope, look here." Delia pointed at a large darkened area on the ground. She walked around it until she found what she was looking for, "Here's the quarrel. That dark spot is where she bled out. See the indentations where her knee and elbow came down?"

Grom sat down. His face was hot, and his eyes felt strange. When he spoke, his voice sounded a bit deeper and raspier than usual, "So she died? Is that what yer sayin'? An' what about our Thomas?"

Delia felt a sudden pang, her own detachment had shielded her from her emotions, but seeing the stalwart dwarf on the verge of tears struck a chord within her. "I don't know Grom, but I don't think she died here. Someone took her body away, probably Thomas himself. He drew the shaft and then carried her off—the trail leads that way. I don't think he would have done all that if she were already dead, but...," she left her statement open as the scene in front of her blurred.

It took them a few minutes to collect themselves, and then they started into the brush, following a cold trail. Delia's tracking skills were good, but she doubted she could have followed such an old trail if it hadn't been for all the blood. *There's so much, there's no way she could have survived that.*

Grom followed her as closely as he could, but his short legs and heavy armor slowed them considerably. The farther they went, the more a sense of urgency built in her.

"I'm going ahead," Delia informed him. "I'll blaze the trail for you to follow." She pulled out a small hatchet to mark the trees and began moving more quickly.

Grom cursed and swore as he tried to keep up, but it was no use. The ranger broke into a graceful sort of lope, and he was left far behind within minutes. *I'm comin' Thomas, don't give up! Don't let her die on us.* It was uncommon for him to pray. Generally, he felt it wasn't worth the time if you didn't have something important to say, but this fit his definition. *I know ye saved me once already, but this ain't fer me. Keep them safe an' I'm yer dwarf, if I wasn't already.*

Delia ran nimbly through the trees, moving like a ghost across the landscape. She was at home again, but it gave her no joy. With catlike grace, she moved effortlessly on, pushing herself ever faster, until she found it difficult to keep following the trail. Her hair was streaming behind her as she ducked low limbs and leapt over rotting logs. She stopped abruptly. *I've lost it. Damnitt!* She swore and began to backtrack, cursing herself for losing time with her excessive haste. Then she heard something, *was that a voice?*

Crouching low, she began slowly stalking toward the sound. *There.* A huge tree rose before her, the sound of soft voices was coming from the other side. She got closer, easing around one side, cautious lest she give herself away.

Seconds later she was sure it was them, and she started to rise from her hiding place. She was within ten yards now, but something stopped her. *Did she say Delia?* Curiosity got the better of her, and she held herself still, straining to hear.

Islana lay on the ground, cushioned by a large mound of moss and leaves. Her face was ashen, but there was no evidence of blood. Thomas sat close by, his robe in tatters, partly from his nighttime journey through the wood, and partly because he'd been cutting rags and bandages from the hem. A small pot was close by, and he brought a wet rag from it as Delia watched, using it to cool Islana's forehead.

"You have to tell her," Islana's voice was soft, barely audible, and it had an airy wheeze to it.

"Of course, I will. Islana you need to rest, you're wearing yourself out," Thomas replied. He looked bad. He still had dried blood on his face and looked as though he'd been badly beaten, purple and yellow bruises adorned his cheek and arms.

Islana ignored his suggestion, "I'm dying Thomas, I don't need rest. There's no point in dragging it out. I'd rather use what time I have to talk. There are too many things I haven't said yet." The words came slowly; she had to work to get enough air out for each phrase.

"Ok fine, but don't waste your breath, you're repeating yourself. And you are *not* dying," said Thomas.

"Tell Delia I'm sorry. I shouldn't have kissed you."

He snorted, "I kissed *you*. You have a fever, you're not making sense. Why would she care about that?" Even fatigue couldn't hide his surprise, though.

"Don't lie, please. It doesn't suit you. I know about it already, she gave me a choice—but I was too scared. I let her..."

Delia was shocked, the woman was dying, next to the man she wanted, and she was feeling guilty because she thought Delia had some sort of claim on him. The very idea was foreign to her concept of human relations. *If he kissed her, why didn't she take what was offered?* It was difficult to name all the emotions that washed over her. Pity and sadness, those were easy to recognize; anger too, that Islana seemed unable to take what had been offered; and jealousy. She herself had been rejected. *Well sort of rejected.* Obviously, Thomas' response to her seduction hadn't been entirely negative.

The ranger became so engrossed in her thoughts, she didn't notice the bear until it was very close. She caught the sound of it snuffling as it drew close to where her friends lay. For a second, she was relieved, it was upwind from her hiding spot, and if she stayed quiet, it would probably pass on without noticing her presence. That wasn't true of Thomas and Islana though, and it seemed to have already caught their scent. Her eyes widened as it moved out of the brush, ambling toward their shelter. Delia had never seen a larger bear. It was a huge boar, all brown fur and rippling muscle, easily twelve hundred pounds or more.

It might not have been a danger, if it wasn't hungry, but that didn't seem to be the case. She could see its excitement, ears perking up as it approached an easy meal. Thomas had seen it now; he was standing, scimitar in hand. He seemed calm, bravely standing his ground, but she could see him swaying. *He can barely stand, much less run,* thought the ranger.

In her mind, she could recall Master Timon's advice to her once, *"The last thing a fool does, is loose an arrow at a grizzly. Don't do it, not unless you're standing on a castle wall, and even then, think it over carefully."*

She was going to run. The bear could have them; nothing was worth being eaten. In her mind, Delia could see herself preparing to take flight. Only a fool would take on such a huge bear in its own domain.

Her body however, had other things in mind. She watched her hands stringing her bow, the task sure and graceful from long practice. She nocked an arrow and drew in a long smooth motion as she stood. So silent had been her draw, that the bear was still unaware, though she stood only twenty feet behind it. The strain on the bow grew as she drew the arrow to its full extension. Softly she exhaled, and when her lungs were empty, she released the string.

The arrow flew true, though she could hardly miss at such close range. Because of the bear's facing, she had no hope of a heart shot, and the skull itself was far too thick to hope for, the arrow wouldn't penetrate. Instead, she took the only target available to her, one that might give her enough advantage to escape the wrath that would ensue. The shaft buried itself deep in the bear's right hind leg, high up, near the hip. Such a wound couldn't possibly kill the massive creature, but it might slow it down, not to mention draw its attention away from her wounded friends.

Time froze as several things happened at once. Thomas' eyes locked with hers for a moment, shock and surprise on his face, followed a second later by fear, as he saw the bear turn toward her. For her own part, she winked at him, masking her own anxiety, and then she began yelling and waving her arms, to ensure the bear knew exactly who had shot it. *Nothing like making sure of a job well done.* The bear meanwhile, screamed out its rage, turning to discover the source of the pain. Then it lunged at her.

Delia wasted no time, sprinting away as fast as her legs could carry her. Glancing over her shoulder, she was awed by the sight of the massive beast surging after her. *How can something that big move so fast?* Weaving in and out among the trees, she tried to gain ground by forcing it to make small turns, but she actually lost more ground. *If I had four legs, I could win this race.* It was so close now she could almost feel its breath at her back, great lungs working like a massive forge billows behind her.

Eyes wide, she scanned the trees ahead, hoping to see what she needed. Too small and it would be over quickly, too large and she might be unable to scale it fast enough. Black bears and young browns could climb quite well, but she knew this monstrosity was far too big to do so.

There! She threw her bow ahead of her, arcing it upwards, hoping it would be trapped in the branches; then she leapt. Her bound carried her up, arms outstretched to catch a lower limb. Using the momentum from her run she swung her body up into the boughs. The next few seconds were a terror, scrabbling and clawing to maintain her perch, but at last she secured her spot, a good fifteen feet from the ground.

Below her the bear reared up, standing and stretching. It was frightening how far it could reach. If she had stopped at ten feet, it might have snared her. Unfortunately, her bow had not stayed in the tree as she had hoped. She could see it lying below, a good ten yards beyond the base of the tree. *I guess adrenaline isn't always a good thing.* If she still had it she might have eventually killed the mammoth bear as it tried to wait her out. *I guess we're in for a long staring contest. Oh well, give it your best Mr. Bear, I can outlast you any day.*

The grizzly had other ideas. The tree itself was a solid ten inches in diameter at the base, not exactly a huge example of the elm family, but surely enough to keep her safe. The tree shook as the bear hurled itself against it, but held firm. After a few tries, the animal changed tactics. Stretching up, it caught a large lower limb and began to lean back, then forward, using its massive weight to whip the trunk back and forth.

Delia grimaced. *Nobody mentioned how smart they are,* she thought to herself.

A sharp crack heralded the demise of an otherwise healthy tree. Popping and splitting the trunk leaned over, while further down some of the bigger roots snapped. Delia was falling. She tried to land on her feet, but limbs struck her as she fell and she wound up landing on her back instead, the air leaving her lungs with a great whoosh.

Stunned, she couldn't recover quickly enough. The beast towered over her, grim and deadly. Delia knew it was over. Then she saw Grom's axe sprout suddenly from the bear's injured leg, sinking into the joint.

The dwarf was roaring, trying to match the bear's ferocity with his own as the axe struck with all the force he could muster, before a wall of fur and claws slammed into him. Grom wasn't tall, but he was close to two hundred pounds, even so, he was flung back like a child's doll, his axe still buried in the flesh of the creature's leg.

The great animal had not given up on his quarry, though. Ignoring the dwarf, it went for Delia, and she might have died then, but its leg collapsed causing it to slip, howling in rage. Using its three good legs, it levered itself up, but then Grom was back. Leaping up he got his strong arms around its huge throat and pulled back, forcing most of its weight over on the one good foreleg on that side.

Grom's face was locked in a rictus grin as he strove with the bear. The bear had only one good hind leg now, and when it raised one foreleg to claw him, he shoved forward, sending them into a roll. He fought to keep his grip around its head, in the meantime, as any slip would give it the freedom needed to bring its jaws to bear.

That turned out to be irrelevant; the roll put him under the bear's shoulder, crushing him against the ground. Ribs snapped and blood erupted from his mouth. His hold on the bear's neck was lost and it quickly righted itself, turning to clamp great jaws upon his shoulder. Waves of pain rolled across him as he felt his collarbone give way.

Grom tried to spit in the beast's eye, but there was no air left in his lungs to propel the bloody spittle. *Eaten by a fucking bear. Me da' would be so proud.* The jaws released his shoulder, most likely to find new purchase on his flesh.

Long seconds passed, but the bear didn't move. Viscous strings of saliva dripped down onto the dwarf's face and the stench of its breath was awful, "Godsdamnitt, either eat me or go home, but stop fuckin' drooling on me!" At least that's what he tried to say, but his broken ribs kept him from making it more than a whisper.

"Grom! Grom! Are you ok?" He could see Delia's slender form climbing over the massive animal's body, bow in hand.

"Do I look ok to ye? I got this wee tiny beastie and the world's heaviest trollop on top o' me! 'Course I'm fine!" again, his words came out far too weakly to have the proper effect.

Thomas found them minutes later, still trying unsuccessfully to shift the animal's weight off the fallen dwarf. He suggested a lever, and with the help of a large limb they finally got the bear off Grom. There were eight arrows deep in its side, two caught in the shoulder bone, one in the fatty lump behind its head. The others were in the ribs and abdomen, one of those had passed between the ribs to pierce the lungs.

Thomas looked at the bear, then at Grom, then Delia.

She cocked her hip and winked at him, "Don't look at me, I'm not cleaning it. *You* can gut and butcher the damn thing."

Thomas laughed, and Grom might have too, if it hadn't hurt so much.

Thomas and Delia helped the injured dwarf hobble back to the tree where Islana lay. After some discussion, they decided the ranger was the obvious choice to return for help, especially since she was the only one who could find her way out, much less back again. Since they were nearer to Weston than Drumaness, she headed for the temple of Delwyn.

"I'll be back as quickly as possible," Delia's concern at leaving her wounded companions alone was evident.

Grom was propped against the stump of the once proud elm, "Don't worry lass, I'll guard them while yer gone." He had regained enough wind to talk after some rest, and he tried to laugh at his own joke, but even that was too much to manage.

Chapter 13
Recovery

Delia returned before noon the next day; Father Whitmire and a small contingent of guards with her. It was good that the abbot himself came; Islana's fever had gotten worse, and without magical aid she would not have survived the trip back to Weston.

The guards built a litter to carry her on. Islana had lost so much blood that even with powerful healing, she was still unable to walk. It would be weeks before she fully regained her strength.

A few days later, Delia paid a visit to Islana's room, ostensibly to bring her flowers. She had found the flowers in a meadow near town, a motley collection of 'brown-eyed susans' and purple coneflowers. Delia took a seat by the bed. She wasn't sure how to say what she wanted, so she just watched the other woman as she fussed over the flowers.

Eventually, Islana got tired of waiting for her, "You look like you've got something you want to talk about."

"Islana, I'm sorry," said the ranger. Their eyes met for a moment, then they both looked away, embarrassed.

"So am I."

"No, wait. Hear me out," Delia continued, "I *am* sorry, very sorry. I'm also a bit put out with you, but let me explain."

Islana interrupted anyway, "You and Grom saved my life. You have nothing to apologize for!"

"Yes, I do, if you'll let me finish," Delia sighed. "I overheard you talking to Thomas, before the bear came. You said you had kissed him so I thought…"

"Delia, I'm sorry. I shouldn't have done that. I knew you and he were intimate…" apologized the paladin.

"Damn it, Islana! Stop apologizing!" Delia shouted. That got Islana's attention, and left her a bit bewildered. Delia took a breath and continued, "Thomas isn't mine! He's not a possession. For that matter, we're not even intimate, well not exactly. I mean, I tried, but he wouldn't— that's not the point. The point is this: You can't spend your life sacrificing your needs. If you want him, do something about it! He can make up his own damn mind what he wants. So, don't tell me that you're sorry! If I had been in your place I would not have stopped at a kiss."

Islana sat, thinking. The combination of advice and revelations had overwhelmed her mind. *So they aren't…,* her thought stopped there, even mentally, she had trouble thinking the word. "Why are you telling me this?" She gave Delia an even, appraising stare.

"Because I couldn't bear watching you blame yourself for this. To be such a strong woman, you spend too much time undermining yourself." Delia looked away, "You deserve better than that."

Islana frowned, "You contradict yourself. You tell me not to sacrifice my needs, but what are you doing now? You say we should take what we want? Then why are you trying to help me?" The paladin held a flower in her fingers, examining the petals.

"I admire you, Islana. You're everything I cannot be, and some things I don't want to be, but you're a good woman, and maybe—maybe a friend. Besides, there are plenty of things you haven't considered; you have such a black and white mindset. Just because a man *fucks* a woman, doesn't forever seal him to her. Even if we *had* taken a tumble, you still could've had some fun in Drumaness."

Islana was blushing furiously and her mouth seemed to be frozen half agape. Unable to resist the fun of tormenting her, Delia continued, becoming more explicit, "After all, a man's seed renews itself. Just like a bull, he might spend it today on one heifer, but soon enough, he has more to spend on a different cow."

The paladin couldn't take any more, "Delia, stop! By the gods, you are such a slut. How can you think like that? Men and women are not beasts!" They argued for while after that, but Islana could not sway Delia's demented world-view. A knock on the door cut short the debate.

"Come in please! Save me!" Islana was only half joking as Thomas stepped inside.

He looked at the two women, sensing something odd in the air, "What were you talking about?"

Islana flushed red and studied the window, while Delia rose to her feet. Walking past Thomas, she whispered, "Wouldn't you like to know?" before smirking wickedly. "You can have the chair, we're done." She left them alone, shutting the door behind her.

Thomas sat down, and he and Islana talked for a while. He kept the conversation on safe topics, such as her recovery, the weather, and how the others were doing. After a few minutes, she decided to take the offensive, "Thomas, about the other evening." They both knew which evening she meant. "I said some things after, and before but—well—I misjudged you."

Thomas didn't argue, "I agree." He was calm, but his eyes had a strange hint of sadness in them.

Keep going, don't give up now... She started again, "What I'm trying to say, is that maybe if you are free sometime, we could have another picnic..." Her words trailed off at the end. *Why is it so hard to say?*

"Islana, wait." His expression was serious, "I can't. I—I've been thinking about things, meditating, and seeking guidance from the goddess."

She frowned, "And she told you no more picnics?"

He knew she was joking, but didn't let it deter him, "No, but looking back, these past few months, I've been distracted. You nearly died a few days ago, and there wasn't a thing I could do to stop it. That's not why I became a cleric."

"You saved my life! You carried me miles through the forest, in the dead of night. You tended me for days. Those are all good things," she countered, but her words didn't have the desired effect.

"During our entire mission, I did little besides think of you. 'Why is she mad?' or 'She looks so beautiful today.' Or 'Maybe I can kiss her.' None of that is what I was supposed to be doing. If I had been focused properly, on my *faith*, on my *training*, on my *mission,* then I might have had the power to save you. Or you might not have been so badly wounded to begin with," Thomas paused.

Islana felt like crying, but her eyes were dry as he continued, "You were magnificent, Islana. Despite terrible odds, you fought with incredible skill. *You* saved us both. While you have progressed, I feel I have been standing still, and it nearly cost you."

She was tired, "Thomas, enough. You've worn me out. I don't agree with you. I will never agree with you. I understand though, so go pray or meditate or whatever it takes to make you feel better."

"I just wanted to explain, so you wouldn't feel...," he caught himself before saying the word, 'rejected'.

"Yeah, yeah, its ok. We're still friends, now let me get some rest." She closed her eyes, willing him out of the room. After a moment, he did leave.

In the days that followed Thomas did not visit again, although Delia did several times. Islana wasn't sure if that pleased her or not. The younger woman had a way of exasperating her that few did. She was friendly enough, but her strange views regarding men and women annoyed Islana, something that Delia seemed to enjoy doing.

Once she was recovered and back to her own training, the young paladin still didn't see much of Thomas. The few times she ran into him in the halls he was cordial and polite, almost diffident. At the morning services his face held a look of concentration, as though he were striving to reach the goddess through sheer mental effort. Islana wasn't sure how she felt about the 'new' Thomas; he had become strange to her, as though he were a different person. Her only consolation was that he had also distanced himself from Delia and even Grom.

"You know what he told me the other day?" Delia was speaking in strident tones. She had convinced Islana to meet her at the forge to talk things over with Grom. "He told me he was 'fasting'. When I asked him what he had given up, he told me 'people'. He's obviously gone off the deep end."

Islana replied, "He blames himself for what happened when we came back from Drumaness. I think he's trying to focus on his faith." She didn't feel like mentioning her own part in his decision. "Did he say anything to you Grom?"

"Nah, but he hasn't come by to help at the forge since that trip to Drumaness. He seems fine though, ye probably should just let him be, he'll sort it out in his own time." Grom didn't like interfering.

Delia replied, "So it's okay for him to avoid everyone and act like a complete stranger?"

"Ya, if that's what it takes," Grom answered, but even he was uneasy with that thought.

Weeks turned into months and little changed. They were all growing, changing, not physically, but inwardly. Grom had made a lot of progress in his training in the guard, and even though he wasn't human, there was talk that one day he might be made an officer. His combat prowess had improved as well, making him a frightening opponent on the sparring field.

Islana's own growth was of a more spiritual nature. Like Thomas, she spent more time praying and meditating, which had rewarded her with a stronger focus, both in combat and in her connection to the divine. Unlike priests, who gained great magical aid from their gods in the form of spells, paladins manifested their powers in a much more physical sense, their bodies becoming vessels that radiated the goddess' power to everyone and everything around them. Although she wasn't to that point yet, she could feel the beginnings of change within herself.

Delia for her part began taking her classes more seriously. Although the temple had nothing to teach regarding the wilds that rangers called home, it did have much to teach her about self-control. Even though Thomas wasn't spending time helping her to read, she began working harder on her own. In spite of herself, she refrained from seducing any more of the temple residents. Whether she found an occasional dalliance with one of the townsmen, well that was no one's business but her own.

Thomas had gained more respect among the clergy and was now leading several of the weekday services. The others often went to those, which seemed to please him, but he never spent time with them afterward. He was now also acting as the abbot's personal assistant, a role with duties beyond those of a simple secretary. It was rumored that he was being groomed for high rank in the future.

Things might have continued like that indefinitely, if events had not swept them up yet again. The first sign that something was wrong broke into Thomas' awareness with the morning bell as he was preparing to go and greet the dawn. On most days, the six o'clock bell was a simple affair. It would ring out six times to indicate the hour; today however it rang repetitively, and he was pretty sure that it was not yet six anyway. It was an alarm.

Rushing out into the courtyard he found a large crowd. The entire temple was in an uproar, giving him the impression of a disturbed ant mound. More people were still coming out of doors and halls, seeking the source of the commotion, much as he was. It seemed to be centered on the main sanctuary, which dominated the center of the complex, so he worked his way in that direction. The entrance into the great central altar was completely blocked by a line of guards and paladins, Islana was among them.

"What's going on?" He had to work to be heard above all the voices as he reached the line.

"I'm sorry Brother, but you cannot go in at this time," Islana replied coolly. She had seen him coming, but the gravity of the situation made her decide to stick to protocol.

Thomas was annoyed, "Hello, it's me, Thomas. Remember me?" He waved his hand in front of her face as though she had lost her sight. One of the guards beside her couldn't help but snicker; few men acted so forward with Islana when she meant business.

She ignored the laugh. *Suddenly, I'm a close acquaintance when it's convenient for him.* She gritted her teeth, "I know very well who you are. We are currently under orders to keep everyone out, except the abbot, the grand master, and the investigation team. No one else may enter without express permission."

"So I take it there has been a crime committed?" he asked.

She didn't answer; she was doing an admirable impression of a stone pillar.

"I'll just wait here then, I have a feeling I may be called for soon." Thomas took a casual pose just a few feet from her. Five or ten minutes passed, and a few messengers came and went, but otherwise no one entered, at last the abbot appeared behind the guards.

"Dame Islana," the abbot called for her.

"Yes, Your Grace?" she said, standing straighter.

"Could you send someone to fetch Thomas for me? He still hasn't shown up and I really need to consult with him. I can't imagine why he hasn't—oh, there you are!" He had spotted Thomas.

"I got here as soon as I could, Your Grace," said Thomas, giving Islana a knowing smile.

"What took you so long? I'd have thought everyone in the place was out there by now."

"I was indisposed, sir. It took me a while to get here." Thomas made no mention of Islana, and he could see she was visibly relieved. The abbot walked him inside. The area around the altar was being thoroughly searched. The source of the tumult was immediately obvious to Thomas; the chalice was not in its accustomed place.

The Chalice of Light was the greatest relic possessed by the temple of Delwyn, and not just in Port Weston, it was the most important relic of all those kept by the various temples to Delwyn in other cities. It had been created over a hundred years ago, by the famous Saint Virgil and was rumored to grant the user, if he dared to attempt it, the power to summon Delwyn herself. It was unique. It was irreplaceable.

To make matters worse, the Festival of Sun was coming up in a few months, a time when the followers of Delwyn traditionally carried the relic with them during a great display, a parade through the streets of Port Weston. If they were unable to show the chalice during the festival it would result in a real loss of face for the temple itself. In some ways Delwyn's reputation was more important than the relic itself.

"When was this discovered?" Thomas asked.

Sir Brevis, the Grand Master of the temple paladins, answered, "Early this morning, when the acolytes came in to prepare the altar for the Dawn Greeting."

"The guards on duty last night saw nothing out of the ordinary," added Abbot Whitmire. "Thomas, I'd like you to meet Captain Bartram, he's the head of the city watch." As he said this, he motioned to the older watchman who had been talking to the temple investigators a moment before.

"Good to meet you, Captain Bartram," Thomas said. "I wish it were on a more pleasant occasion."

The watchman had a discerning face, and he looked Thomas over for a moment, "The Abbot has had good things to say about you, Brother Thomas. Do you have any ideas?"

"No sir, I'm a novice in these matters, I fear he overrates my abilities."

They discussed the implications of the theft for some time, but got nowhere. No one had seen anything, the guards were cleared of suspicion, and no trace or clue was to be found in the altar chamber itself. In short, they were completely stumped. The investigation team's divinations had found very little as well, other than traces of abjuration magics.

Whitmire summed things up, "So to restate things, the guards weren't tampered with, as far as we can tell. Many of the powerful wards guarding the altar itself were bypassed using primarily mundane means, which is unusual. I would normally suspect a powerful wizard, considering the protections here, but that seems not to be the case. It appears this was done by a skilled thief, using only such magics as were required to hide his presence and prevent us from tracking him after the fact."

"You suggest that the thieves' guild was involved," said Sir Brevis. The senior paladin had little trouble believing that. The city guard had an informal arrangement with the leader of Port Weston's shady crime organization, but the paladin had never condoned it.

Father Whitmire shook his head, "I suggest nothing. I do, however, think that we should start our questioning there. Whoever did this was very skilled. Whether they were affiliated with John Small or not, he should have some knowledge of them." John Small was the erstwhile leader of the city's thieves' guild. Thomas had never heard him mentioned before.

Bartram spoke up, "I can probably arrange a meeting with him if you like. The watch occasionally has to deal with him for information."

Whitmire gave the captain a knowing glance, "That would be appreciated."

The Abbot continued, "Thomas, I have a task for you. I want you to take a team, some of the younger, more energetic members of the temple. If the Captain can arrange a meeting with John Small this evening; you'll take it from that point."

"Excuse me, Your Grace?" Thomas was in shock.

"Trouble with your hearing?" asked Whitmire.

"No sir, but why me?" returned Thomas, there was no point in beating around the bush.

"Thomas, you performed well a few months ago in trying circumstances. I trust you. You're young, and you show promise. Something like this could well be a stepping stone for you. Enough with the self-doubt, who would you choose to help you?" Father Whitmire's eyes bored into him.

After a moment, Thomas answered, "Grom, Brother Tashley, and Walter." He didn't blink as he listed the names.

"That was quick. A warrior, a young priest and a paladin trainee, not a bad mix, but I wonder that you chose those particular individuals. Why not include the ranger, Delia? Her skills would be most useful, rather than another priest. You've worked together before, she would seem ideal," said Father Whitmire.

"Your logic is sound, Your Grace, perhaps I will consider her in place of Tashley then," Thomas tried to hide his discomfiture at the suggestion.

But the Abbot wasn't finished, "And why choose Walter? He's not taken his vows yet."

"He's promising, a quick fighter, and I trust him," Thomas replied.

"You don't trust Dame Islana?" The Abbot was remarkably perceptive.

"I do sir, but that's not the problem."

"She's taken her vows. She's twice the fighter Walter is, and you've worked with her before. I don't see the logic in choosing someone else. Is this personal?" Thomas took a deep breath, "Yes sir." *Not only will they distract me, but now I might face seeing my friends hurt once again.*

"Get over it," Whitmire stated bluntly. "Delwyn has no time to wait for you to resolve your personal issues." That effectively ended the debate.

After leaving the room Thomas began making arrangements. Returning to the abbot's study, he quickly penned messages to those who were to accompany him, giving them to the cantor on duty to deliver to his friends. It was going to be a long day.

CHAPTER 14
MOR DAI MELGEHM

That evening Thomas waited outside the Abbot's study until his friends arrived. Their faces were serious as they looked at him.

Delia was the first to speak, "You look like you swallowed a frog. Are you going to tell us what we're here for?"

"The Abbot will do that in a moment, it's better if I let him explain." Thomas answered.

Islana looked at him, "About earlier, I'm sorry that was…"

"It's ok," Thomas interrupted, "Let's go in, we shouldn't keep them waiting." Opening the door, Thomas went into the Abbot's study, the others filing in behind. Father Whitmire sat behind his desk, with Captain Bartram across from him in a chair. A third man stood to one side. He was unfamiliar to Thomas, not that it would have made much difference, he wore a masked cowl which covered his head and upper face. The material appeared to be black silk, which matched the broad brimmed hat he wore on his head. The rest of his clothing was similarly black, dark leather matched by an ebon cloak. Thomas noted that he also wore a rapier.

Whitmire looked up at their entrance, "Oh good timing." Glancing at Thomas he gestured to the watch captain, "You met Captain Bartram earlier, this is one of his acquaintances—a man he assures me has a rare combination of talents." The Abbot went on to introduce each of them to the watch officer. "Captain, why don't you introduce your associate?"

Bartram nodded, "This is a fellow who's been most useful to the watch in the past, although he has no official connection, Mor Dai Melgehm."

The masked stranger stepped forward at that, "Glad to make your acquaintance." His voice was dry, almost masking the cultured tones of a nobleman. He stood about five foot, six inches tall, with a slim to moderate build and aquiline features. Not much could be seen of his hair but his sideburns were black, offsetting his sharp blue eyes.

Bartram continued, "Mor Dai has agreed to arrange a meeting with John Small."

Islana spoke up, "Your grace, if you don't mind my asking, we still don't know why we're here."

"I seem to have gotten ahead of myself," the Abbot said, "I thought Thomas might have already explained. I've assigned Thomas the task of finding and recovering the Chalice of Light. After some discussion, he and I decided you three would be ideal to assist him with this mission."

"Your Grace," Islana said, "if you don't mind my asking, doesn't this seem like something that should be handled by more senior representatives?"

Whitmire responded, "Dame Islana, you took your oaths to serve the goddess. In her eyes we are all but children. This task is being set upon Thomas' shoulders;

your task is to make sure that he does not fail. Do you feel you will be unable to meet your vows?"

"I will do everything I am able to fulfill them, Your Grace." Islana felt she had been backed into a corner.

"Can we trust you to keep to your part in this, Mor Dai?" Delia surprised them with her interruption.

"I can only do as I have said and take you to meet John. As to how he responds, I am unable to predict. I don't work for him. I merely help him from time to time." The dark clad man's words were sobering.

Grom stared at the masked man with open suspicion, "If ye don't work for him, and ye don't work for the watch, who do ye work for? I ken ye not." It was a question on all of their minds.

Bartram moved to defend Mor Dai, "This man has done me many good turns in the past. As far as I can tell he moves to his own tune, but he has never lied to me yet. You can trust him."

Mor Dai held up a hand. "I understand your concerns; this mask does little to inspire trust. If you will let me explain…," he paused for a moment, waiting to see if anyone would interrupt, then seeing their patient gazes he continued, "I lead a simple life, one I would protect. Yet my conscience compels me to lead a dual existence. This mask protects my regular life, and those that I share it with from my actions in the night. I have my reasons, but I will ask you to accept me on that. I can offer no more."

Islana glared at him, "You're a vigilante."

Thomas had been studying the masked man as he talked, and something about him made Thomas believe him, in spite of his mask. Trusting his instincts, Thomas spoke, "If the watch captain vouches for you, then that's good enough for me. When can we meet with John?"

"An hour from now. I started making arrangements as soon as the captain contacted me," Mor Dai answered.

After that they cut short their discussion while everyone got ready. Most of them already had their gear and weapons, but it still took them a few minutes to gather their things and meet at the front gate. The meeting was to take place at a seedy dive known as "The Blue Mermaid", one of the most disreputable taverns in Port Weston, located near the wharves, as the name would suggest.

When they entered the tavern Thomas felt sure that Mor Dai's unusual appearance would garner more attention than it did. Oddly enough most of the customers accepted his strange dress easily enough, either from experience or simple caution. The black garbed Mor Dai led them to the bar where a small bald man stood waiting. The man looked at Mor Dai and then gave the rest of them an appraising glance, "The boss is waiting upstairs, first door on the left." He turned back to his drink and studiously ignored their presence. Mor Dai led them up the stairs.

The upstairs hallway was empty, but the seedy tavern made Thomas nervous, he put his hand on Mor Dai's shoulder before he knocked on the door, "One second." Turning, he looked at the others, "Delia, go back down to the bar and keep watch. If anything unusual happens, let us know."

The ranger winked at him and headed back downstairs.

Once she was gone, Thomas turned to the others, "Grom, I want you to guard the door, Islana and I will go in with Mor Dai."

"Ye're just afraid they'll swoon at me dwarven good looks!" Grom's words were mocking, but the look in his eye was serious, he loosened his axe and put his back to the wall.

Mor Dai put his hand on the door, "You don't have to worry, John is many things, but he hasn't double crossed me yet. This meeting is almost as safe as one back in the temple." With that he led them into a small room, where a man sat at a table, idly shuffling a deck of cards.

John was unassuming in appearance; of medium build, slender with a hint of the athletic about him. His features and clothing were nondescript, unkempt red hair and hazel eyes failed to make him stand out, but his presence filled the small, dimly lit room. Something about him hinted that he was not a man to be trifled with, although Thomas would have been hard pressed to put a finger on what made him feel that way.

He seemed to be alone, but after a second glance around the room Thomas realized he was not, a rather large man stood quietly in the corner. A single chair sat across the table from John, and he motioned towards it, "Sit down, let's see if we can help each other."

"Perhaps I should stand." Thomas answered, "There don't seem to be enough chairs for all of us."

"I prefer to stand," Mor Dai said.

Glancing at his companions, Thomas noticed that Islana's stance was tense, and her hand was resting on the hilt of her sword. She shook her head to indicate her preference to stand. Rather than make things more awkward, Thomas took the seat and wasted no time getting to business, "I assume you know why we're here."

"'Assuming', now that has a lot to do with why I'm here." John's voice had an odd lilt to it, faintly reminiscent of a Drumaness accent, but actually quite different. "I know what you're lookin' for, but as ta where and how, I'm as clueless as you lot."

Thomas pushed on, "Captain Bartram said you might be able to help set us on the right path to recover the Chalice."

"Yeah, that's why I'm here. Obviously a lot of people are gonna be wonderin' who nicked it, and just as surely some of 'em are gonna be thinkin' o' me and my crew. But I had nothin' ta do with it. I'm hopin' ye find it soon, otherwise its goin' ta be hard to keep my crew workin' in this town." John's tone was casual, but his eyes were hard. It was clear that he took the matter quite seriously.

Thomas thought carefully, "So we find the Chalice, and you're in the clear."

"That sounds about right, mate. The only trouble is—I don't have a clue where ya should start. I've been suspectin' for some time that there's another crew in town, but they're real smart. I've had me boys lookin' for 'em, but so far we haven't been able to find 'em. It's like they don't exist. Either that or they're real good." John seemed at a loss.

Thomas listened carefully, watching the other man's face. He had a good ear for lies, but John seemed to be telling the truth. Still he couldn't trust that, in all likelihood John was a consummate liar, given his line of work. "As I see it we have two problems. One, we need a place to start looking. Two, once we start looking, how are we going to be able to tell your men from those working for someone else?"

John's face took on a thoughtful expression and he leaned back in his chair, his cards forgotten for a moment. "If Mor Dai is with you, he should know most of me boys, otherwise you can always send a runner to check with me. Leavin' that aside, there's been some commotion up the north road. My crew works in town, whoever's workin' up that way is sure to not be part o' me or mine."

Thomas leaned forward, "What do you mean by 'commotion'?"

"I guess ye haven't heard about it, but there's been a number of wagons robbed on the north road. Worse, they ain't just robbin' 'em. Whoever's been at it hasn't been leaving witnesses, if ye get my meanin'."

Thomas thought for a moment, "Alright, we'll look into it; see if we can shake anything loose from the trees. If you discover anything in the meantime, will you let us know?"

"'Course, it's as much in my interest as yours to see this taken care of quickly," said John, before picking up the cards and riffling them again. Thomas got up and took his leave.

They gathered outside the tavern and stopped for a moment to discuss their options. "We'll head back to the temple for tonight. We can set out along the north road in the morning." Thomas told them. "Mor Dai, will you be able to meet us around seven a.m.?"

The masked man looked uncertain for a moment, "Sure, I'll have to make a few arrangements, but I can manage that." It was about this time that they heard a woman's cry from an alley nearby. Whoever she was she was clearly in distress, but her scream was cut short by a sickening thump, as if she had been struck hard.

Islana and Delia exchanged questioning glances, startled for a moment, then they saw Thomas and Mor Dai running for the alley. "Stop!" Thomas yelled at the entrance to the alleyway, addressing a group of men who held a young woman in the shadows.

One of them turned and addressed the cleric and Mor Dai, the others had not yet come into their view, "Now, I'd think it would be better for all concerned if you two lads turned and walked away. Go find your own wench; we're not of a mind to share tonight." The thug had an evil grin, his lips contorted into a smirk.

Thomas started to address him, "I'm afraid we can't...," but his reply was cut short by Mor Dai's loud challenge.

"Stand and deliver!" The street avenger had already unsheathed his rapier and was striding rapidly toward the men. Thomas felt the air move as Islana and Grom ran past him, while Delia stopped beside him and brought out her bow.

This is about to turn into a bloodbath. Thomas thought to himself. The time for words was done, however. The man who had spoken to them brought out a wicked blade as Mor Dai approached. Two of the others released the girl and drew daggers and clubs, preparing to fight as well. The fourth kept a firm grip on the girl.

Things moved quickly from there, Mor Dai was in among them and his rapier was already red with blood. The first man was still crumpling to the ground clutching his belly as Mor Dai approached the other two, Grom and Islana close behind him. The last two fought viciously but were no match for the three seasoned fighters, but even as they struggled, the fourth man realized things weren't going well. He shoved the girl aside and brought out a long knife, preparing to gut her and run before his companions were overcome.

Flames lit the scene for a moment, as a bolt of fire leapt from Thomas' hands, striking him full in the face. Screaming, he dropped the knife, batting at his burning hair before suddenly falling to the ground. His neck had sprouted one of Delia's arrows. Almost as quickly as it had started, it was over. Four men lay sprawled on the cobblestones; all but one already dead, and the last one didn't look as if he would survive long without quick attention.

The girl they had been accosting sat on the ground, her back against the wall, her face blank. She seemed to be in shock. Thomas approached her slowly; afraid he might frighten her more, "It's alright, we're here to help. Are you hurt anywhere?"

Blinking she looked up at him, for a moment she seemed uncomprehending, but then her reserve broke, and she began to cry. Standing suddenly, she threw herself into Thomas' arms, sobbing. "Oh thank the gods! I thought they were going to kill me, or—or—but you... Thank you!" Her tears were flowing freely but Thomas couldn't help but be aware of her soft form pressed against him.

This isn't quite how I imagined this scenario, he thought. In truth, although she was a damsel in distress, she was anything but beautiful. Mousy brown hair hung loosely about her shoulders, and her face was extremely plain, if not homely, despite her young age. The girl continued to thank him, and he began to grow embarrassed, after all his part in her rescue had been quite small. Behind him he could hear Delia speaking to Islana. "And here I thought you were the only competition," she said this with a barely hidden laugh.

Mor Dai stepped in and addressed the girl, and Thomas was glad for the distraction, "Ma'am, if you don't mind, could you tell us your name and where you live? We'd be glad to escort you home."

She looked up from Thomas' shoulder but kept a firm grip on him, "It's Darcy, sir. My mom's going to kill me for being out too late." She lowered her eyes for a moment, before raising them again to stare at Thomas, "But you saved me, you—and your friends. I can't tell you how grateful I am."

Thomas was beginning to get an idea of how the girl had wound up in her previous predicament. She seemed extremely naïve, and entirely too quick to put her trust in strange men. "It was nothing," he replied. "Nothing any decent folk wouldn't do. Now if you'll just tell us where you live, we'll make sure you get back safe tonight."

"I live by the tannery, a few streets over, it isn't far. I don't mind if you walk me, but you needn't trouble your friends..." She was gazing at Thomas with an uncomfortably intent stare.

Just then a whistle sounded and several of the town watch ran up, "Everyone hold! What's going on here?" The speaker was a young watchman with blond hair and an honest face. Thomas glanced around at his friends. Grom stood by silently, bloody axe still in his hands, Delia was near him with a casual stance, no trace of anxiety about her. Islana was next to Thomas, tense, and though he couldn't see it, he knew her hand was near her sword. Mor Dai had vanished like a shadow.

"My name is Deacon Thomas, of the temple of Delwyn. We were just coming down the street when we heard this young lady calling for help over..."

"He saved me! They all did, them ruffians were beating on me something fierce because I didn't want to give them what they wanted, when these kind folk appeared and stopped them." Naturally, she was still clinging to Thomas like a lost child, but her story was helped by the visible swelling of her lip and cheek. She'd likely have a nasty bruise in the morning.

"Ok slow down, I'll want the details from each of you, one at a time," said the watchman. He nodded at Thomas, "If you'd be so kind as to start."

"Certainly, Sergeant...," Thomas let the words trail off, "...I'm sorry I haven't gotten your name yet."

"Wilkins, Corporal Wilkins." The watchman replied. It took them a good half hour to relay all the details to him, even though the fight itself had taken no more than a minute or so. In the end, the watchman was satisfied, if not impressed.

"I'm glad you lot were here. We could use more citizens like yourselves. I'll be glad to see that the girl gets home safely, but would you mind dropping by the watch house in the morning to make a deposition?" He seemed genuine in his thanks.

Thomas frowned, "I'll do my best, Corporal, but I have important duties to attend to for the church. It might be a few days before I'm free."

Wilkins regarded him somberly, "I'd advise you to come in as soon as possible. My report will show this as an act of civic duty, but should anyone present a grievance for these men, the magistrate might change that to a possible homicide if you don't present your side in person."

"I'll keep that in mind," said Thomas.

After the watchmen had left, with the reluctant Darcy in tow, Mor Dai apologized, "I fear my actions may have brought you trouble. I hope this doesn't delay your mission."

Thomas let his eyes sweep across the others, from Islana, to Grom, to Delia. None of them would have done any differently, even had Mor Dai not leapt into action first. "None of us could have ignored that, Mor Dai. The blame is not yours."

CHAPTER 15
THE SAINTS

Thomas slept fitfully that night.

Abbot Whitmire had decided to mobilize the temple guard the next morning, since facing a potentially large and dangerous band of outlaws was beyond the scope of what their small group could be expected to handle. It seemed Thomas' deposition at the guard headquarters would have to wait.

Despite his anxiety, Thomas went to sleep almost as soon as he put head to pillow. When he opened his eyes again he expected to see the first light of dawn peeping in through his window, but instead he saw only a dimly lit room.

A room that was not his own.

He tried to sit up, only to discover he was already standing. Around him were rough-hewn stone walls. On one side stood an iron door, with no window or handle. Runes marked the stone on every side, though they were hard to see. Their color was a midnight black, so dark they seemed to swallow whatever light reached them.

Turning around, he found the source of light, a young girl sat in the middle of the floor, radiating a warm glow no brighter than that of a candle. Iron manacles encased her wrists and ankles, fastening her cruelly to the floor with iron chains. Red-gold hair covered her face, but when she looked up it fell away, allowing Thomas to see her features. He knew her.

"Sarah!" he gasped.

"Thomas," she said softly, her voice almost a whisper. "I'm so sorry."

He tried to go to her, but he quickly discovered his body would not move. He was stuck in place, like a fly in amber. "Why are you apologizing to me?" he asked. "You're the one in chains. What happened?"

She smiled sadly at him, "Don't fear for me, Thomas. Things are as they had to be. I only wish I could have given you more time."

"I don't understand."

"Tomorrow you must find me," she told him. "The bandits are only a distraction. Ignore them. You must go south."

"How will I find you?" he asked worriedly. "Half the world lies south of here…"

"Listen to your heart, it will tell you when you are near," she answered. "You will meet a man who will guide you; follow where he leads, but do not trust him."

Thomas frowned in puzzlement, "If I shouldn't trust him, why would I follow him?"

Sarah looked down, "Because he is my ally in this, not yours. He shares the same goal, but given the chance, he would destroy you."

He strained to get closer, but try as he might his body would not move. He wanted to free her, to hold her. Thomas felt the distance separating them as though it were a physical pain in his chest. "How will I know him?" he asked in desperation. "What does he look like?"

The chains that held her were beginning to glow with heat, and smoke rose from Sarah's flesh. It was an acrid smell that burned Thomas's nose. Despite her suffering, Sarah's face remained smooth, "I do not know what appearance he has chosen, but it doesn't matter. He is looking for you. Head south and he will find you."

Frustration threatened to overwhelm him. Thomas wanted to scream, but he fought hard to keep his self-control. "How will I recognize him?"

Sarah lifted one hand, reaching toward him, and the metal at her wrist began glowing more forcefully. The skin around it was turning black. "The paladins will know him..."

And then the world shattered, splintering like broken glass. Sitting up, Thomas found himself in his bed once more, his face covered in sweat. The window was still dark, morning had not yet arrived, but he could sleep no longer.

The dream had seemed real, it *felt* real, but he didn't know what to think of it. Standing, he put on his nightrobe. Dawn was close, he might as well take advantage of the temple bath to wash himself one last time before setting out. He wanted to dismiss the dream, but as he prepared to step out of the room he smelled it one more time, the scent of burning flesh.

"Are you sure?" asked Father Whitmire. "This wasn't just a nightmare?"

"No, Father," answered Thomas.

The Abbot looked at Sir Brevis, "We will do as he suggests then."

The Grand Master's mouth opened in shock, "You would ignore the only lead we have in favor of a—a dream?!"

Whitmire nodded, "It is my decision to make."

The paladin's eyes narrowed, "Only in time of peace, in times of war my authority supersedes yours."

"This is not a time of war," said the Abbot calmly.

"The chalice has been stolen!" protested Sir Brevis. "We are about to send out a military force to recover it. I could easily argue that we *are* in a time of war."

Whitmire arched one brow, "But you won't. You are going to do as young Thomas asks."

Sir Brevis glared at him, "Why?"

Father Whitmire addressed Thomas, "Bare your chest for the Grand Master."

"What?" said Thomas, startled.

"Show him your chest."

"But, Your Grace…," Thomas started to argue.

"Do it."

Red-faced, Thomas removed his robe and pulled his undertunic over his head. He was sensitive about showing his strange birthmark to others. He knew what it looked like now, but he didn't understand why it was pertinent to their discussion.

The paladin's eyes grew wide as he took in the strange mark on Thomas' chest. "By Saint Virgil!" he swore loudly.

"Exactly," replied Whitmire dryly. "What will you do now, Master of Paladins?"

Brevis answered immediately, "We ride south."

The Grand Master left the room to hurry his men along in their preparations, but Thomas stayed behind with the abbot. He began pulling his overtunic back on, but his mind was full of questions, "If this mark is so important, why hadn't you told him about it before?"

Father Whitmire leveled a calm gaze at him, "I've only told two about your *stigma*, Brother Jenkins, and now Sir Brevis. I felt it best to keep it a secret."

"Even from the Grand Master?"

The older priest stood and walked to the window, clasping his hands behind his back. "How much have you learned about the saints?"

The sudden change of subjects took Thomas off-guard, "We studied them under Brother Jenkins, but there were so many…"

The sun was dawning over the temple wall, casting Whitmire's face in stark relief, "Your orphan girl, Sarah, didn't teach you about them? I gathered she lectured you rather extensively about theology."

Thomas had no idea where this was leading, but he answered simply, "No, Your Grace."

"I suppose that makes sense."

"Only if you explain it," said Thomas sourly.

"Do you know how one becomes a saint?"

"The senior priests hold a conclave, usually after the prospective candidate's death and vote on whether…," he began.

"Not that," interrupted Whitmire. "That's how *we* recognize them, but we have a number of criteria that are examined when making that decision. Lifetime service, achievements, and frequently martyrdom, those are some of the most important things we consider, but what most laymen don't realize, is that more than half of those chosen have a stigma similar to yours. Sometimes it isn't discovered until their bodies are examined after death, but whether before or after, it carries great weight in the deliberations."

"You keep calling it a stigma. I thought it was a birthmark," said Thomas.

"It's a sign from our Lady...," said the priest. "...a sign of favor, of blessing, and perhaps a curse as well."

Thomas frowned, "How would a sign from Delwyn be a curse?"

The Abbott turned to face him, "Do you remember how Saint Virgil died? He was a martyr, tortured for seven days while he refused to give up the location of the Chalice of Light to our enemies. He bore the same mark you do, although his was on his lower back. Almost without exception, the men and women who have borne that mark eventually became martyrs, and most of them died painful deaths."

"But not all of them, right?" asked Thomas hopefully.

Whitmire laughed ruefully, "Study their lives if you want to lose sleep at night. The mark you bear is a blessing, a sign of hope to those of us who follow Delwyn, but for those who bear it, it should be considered a warning."

"I'm starting to wish I hadn't asked," said Thomas.

"Would you forsake Her service?" asked Father Whitmire. "If you could avoid whatever lies in store for you and live a quiet and happy life, would you choose to turn your back on Her?"

He gave it serious thought for a moment, but it didn't take him long. Thomas could still remember the day he had sworn fealty to Sarah. He hadn't known she was a goddess then, but the image of her, with the sunlight streaming through her hair had been burned into his mind. There was no uncertainty in his voice when he answered, "No."

"Then we should go down and make ready to ride south. We have a long day ahead of us."

CHAPTER 16
ROAST PIG

The weather was sunny, and the air warmed quickly as they rode from Port Weston along the South road. Thomas began to sweat during the first hour and he felt sorry for Islana. It had to be even hotter in the armor she wore, though she gave little sign of it.

They rode in the largest company Thomas had ever been a part of, twenty men at arms and nine paladins together with seven priests, if you excluded the Abbot, the Grand Master, and his friends from the count.

Grom and Islana were both expected to remain in their respective places within the small column of riders, but Delia was under no such constraint. Riding along the right side of the group, she nudged her horse into a canter and caught up to where Thomas rode near the front. She ignored a few odd looks from the priests as she drew close to him, "I can understand everyone else that's here, but why is *he* riding with us?"

Her eyes and a gesture with her thumb indicated the target of her question, Mor Dai Melgehm. The masked vigilante rode at the rear of the group, conspicuous in the fact that he fit in with none of the other riders.

Thomas shrugged, "When I told him we weren't going north to check out the bandits he said he would ride with us anyway."

"But why did the Abbot allow it?" she wondered aloud.

"I gave a good report of him yesterday but...," began Thomas.

"Delia," interrupted Sir Brevis. "Ride forward a mile or two and see what the road is like."

She pursed her lips sourly but obediently kicked her horse into a fast trot, leaving the group behind. Once she was out of earshot, Whitmire and Brevis exchanged glances before the paladin spoke again, "If we've got a ranger with us we might as well make use of her and scout ahead."

Thomas listened but didn't comment. The road they were on was well traveled and unlikely to offer any surprises. He doubted the senior paladin's decision had been because of any real need for scouting.

Delia didn't particularly like the leader of the temple paladins. In her opinion Sir Brevis was pompous and self-important. In fact, she felt pretty much the same about the rest of the paladins, they were entirely too stuffy. Other than Islana, she didn't have much use for any of them.

Even so, she felt much better once the sounds of the other riders fell away into the distance. Solitude suited her far better than being in a large company. Leaning forward she stroked her mount's neck. She hadn't had a lot of experience with horses, but she had known early on that she liked them better than most people. Horses were pragmatic.

"Isn't that right, Biscuit?" she asked, directing her question to her mount.

Biscuit turned her head slightly, rolling one eye back to look at her rider and then slowed her pace. Clearly haste was no longer required.

Delia smiled, "You are entirely practical. There's nothing mysterious about what you're thinking." She could almost read the animal's mind. Biscuit was wondering when she'd be allowed to stop and have a go at the sweet grass beside the road.

Turning her attention back to the task at hand, Delia studied the dirt ahead. The road was well maintained, but unpaved. Down the middle the dirt was barren and hard packed where a multitude of horse drawn carts and wagons had kept the weeds from growing. Farther from the center a bit of sad grass grew, hardy stuff that had managed to survive the wheels of passing wagons carrying produce to market. Beyond that the roadside grass grew tall; it only had to contend with a yearly cutting from the maintenance crews.

She couldn't tell much from the center of the road. It was too hard to show much. She studied the grass instead. Any recent passages might leave signs there, leaving bent trails through the grass.

Sure enough, she found the telltale sign of a wagon's passage, not that that meant anything, "Probably a farmer smuggling a nefarious load of turnips into the city." Delia snorted. *What do they think I'm going to find out here?*

Still, she continued to study the road. After a short while she knew that the latest wagon had been leaving the city, rather than heading toward it, based on direction that the grass was bent. She kept her ears open, but there was nothing unusual to be heard. The forest around her was quiet, other than the occasional bit of birdsong.

Several miles went by, and at some point, she realized the wagon trail had vanished. There hadn't been any obvious roads or trails diverging from the one she traveled, so she thought it odd. Reining in Biscuit, she turned her mount around and headed back, watching the verges of the road more carefully. Delia spotted the turnoff after traveling less than a hundred yards.

The trees grew differently there, crowding around and over a long unused trail. Delia dismounted and looped Biscuit's reins over a low hanging limb. "Enjoy your snack," she told the horse who had already begun cropping the tall grass.

They stopped here, she noted mentally. The earth was torn and disturbed in places. At a guess, she thought they must have stopped briefly before continuing on into the forest itself. Circling the area, she looked for signs and was eventually rewarded with a partial boot print.

"Someone jumped down here," she said quietly. "Maybe the driver?" The ground was still pretty firm, but the heel had made a deep impression, and that, combined with its width, told her that the farmer had been a large man. "But why did he take his wagon in there?" she wondered.

A few of the smaller branches had been broken, indicating the passage of the wagon. She might have been tempted to think the farmer had been heading for some isolated homestead, but the state of the underbrush told her that the old trail had been unused for a long time. This was the first time anyone had traveled it in quite a while.

Delia's suspicions were fully aroused. She was tempted to take the horse, but she decided she could make better time on foot. Taking her bow from where it was tied to her saddle she strung it and set off. Her steps were light as she jogged into the forest, her feet settling into old patterns as she avoided fallen limbs or ducked beneath low hanging branches.

She wasn't silent as she ran, something like that would have been impossible at that speed, but the noise she made blended in with the forest, no greater or more noticeable than the sound of the wind through the trees, or a squirrel rustling through the ground litter, seeking an acorn.

Delia continued running until a stray breeze brought the smell of something cooking to her nose. *Pig?* She couldn't be sure, but whatever it was made her mouth water. She stopped and waited for the wind to favor her again, making note of its direction. *That way,* she thought. She knew from experience that judging distance from smell alone was nearly impossible, but given the circumstances, she thought there must be a camp nearby. Slowing her pace, she began to pick her way more stealthily through the brush.

The campfire turned out to be closer than she expected. After less than fifty yards she found it, nestled in a shallow depression in the land. Those who had made it had cleared away the brush for ten feet in each direction. The wagon was on the far side from where she approached and three large men were gathered around the fire.

Using greenwood, they had fashioned a heavy rack and spit to roast their kill over, but it was no pig, the shape was wrong. With horror Delia realized that the body skewered above the hot coals was that of a thin man, or perhaps a woman. It was no longer possible to be sure. They had skinned their prey before impaling it, and the fire had already seared the tender flesh beyond easy identification.

Her stomach flipped over, and Delia fought the urge to vomit. She was no more than twenty yards away, and any strange noise or sudden movement might give her away. Sitting down she took several slow deep breaths before looking at them again. When she did, she kept her eyes off the centerpiece over the fire, whoever it was, was already dead.

She saw now that her first impression had been wrong. It was three orcs gathered around the fire, and a fourth, much smaller figure was tied to the wagon. A child.

She had an arrow nocked and drawn before she knew what she was doing, but caution reasserted itself before she released. The orcs were armored and heavy-set. She couldn't be sure of a killing shot. The distance and terrain favored her, but it was unlikely she could kill all three before they reached her. She needed help.

Relaxing the tension in her arm, she started to put the arrow away when again her nose alerted her; a pungent smell of rust and sweat. Turning, she saw the orc's hand-axe sweeping down at her barely in time to roll to one side.

She had not seen the orc lookout as she approached, but by chance she had stopped close to his original position, and he had certainly noticed her. He bellowed a warning for his companions as he swung the axe a second time.

Being on the ground, with a larger, stronger opponent already attacking meant Delia had few options. She couldn't continue her roll; the bushes around her wouldn't permit it. The arrow she had had a moment before was gone, so she did the only thing she could, sweeping her bow sideways, she tried to catch the orc's leg.

His stance was solid, though, and his mass made him practically immovable for her, but the move made him pause to laugh. His humor ended abruptly when Delia's long-knife went through his boot, however. Swinging wildly, he caught the girl with the side of the axe as she tried to rise, sending her falling back through the brush.

Delia recovered from her fall faster than the orc could follow with his wounded foot. Springing up from the ground, she dashed away, leaving her bow and knife behind. She was unarmed now, and her only hope lay in reaching the church knights before the orcs caught up with her.

A chase ensued, and the three orcs from the camp soon outpaced their lamed lookout. They were fast, much faster than Delia had expected such large warriors could be, but they were still no match for her in the forest. She raced through the woods ahead of them like a wraith, nimbly leaping over some groundcover and sliding beneath tangles of vine and thorns that threatened to snare her. By the time she reached her horse she was more than fifty yards ahead of them, though she lost much of that distance while she untied Biscuit and leapt into the saddle.

"What's that?" asked the Abbot, looking ahead. The road stretched out before them, and in the distance, he could see a figure emerging from the brush on one side.

Sir Brevis squinted against the sun, "I think it's our scout."

"Something's wrong," said Islana, speaking over her superiors. She could see Delia was already whipping her horse to gain speed. The ranger was riding as though she had the very demons of hell behind her. A second later she saw the heavy forms of three armored men burst from the trees.

Brevis had noted it as well. Holding up a hand to stop the column he addressed his paladins, "Ready lances!"

The well-trained knights rode forward two steps and lowered their long weapons, but Islana had already kicked her destrier into motion. Sir Brevis swore as she broke formation, "Damnitt!" Looking at his men he yelled, "After her, charge!"

Their horses broke into a trot and began to speed up, but they were almost immediately outpaced as Mor Dai Melgehm shot past them on his speedy courser.

Rapier in hand he raced toward the enemy, "Stand and deliver!"

Thomas watched him go, "I wonder if he realized that line doesn't make any sense at the moment?"

The Abbott ordered the rest of the men to start forward, at a fast pace, but nothing like a charge. The distance between them and the charging paladins widened by the second.

Thomas rose close to the warriors, looking over at Grom, "Shouldn't we be going faster?"

The dwarf, who was riding uncomfortably on a sturdy pony, answered, "Might be a trick, lad. Best we move at a steady pace. If things turn bad we can support them, if not we'll be there in time to mop up after they get their glory."

Ahead of them all, Islana raced toward Delia and the orcs, her hair streaming behind her. She hadn't couched her lance yet, but there was a considerable distance left to cover. Reaching back, she pulled her helm loose from where it had been tied and settled it over her head. She wouldn't be able to fasten the strap while riding like that, but she figured it was better than nothing. Then she lowered her point and leaned forward.

The orcs had already realized their mistake as they saw the knights bearing down on them with lances in hand. As one they broke off their chase and turned back to run for the cover of the forest. Two of them made it, but the third was only seconds from safety when Islana's lance went through his back. The shock of the blow tore the weapon from her grasp, but she continued onward, trying to get her horse through the thick undergrowth to pursue her enemies.

Mor Dai pulled up beside her and vaulted from the saddle, "It'll be quicker on foot!"

Delia had turned her horse around and dismounted as well, "They've taken a child." Those were her only words before she too charged into the dense wood.

Islana was close behind, on foot now. In her armor, she was no match for Mor Dai's speed as he wove in and out through the brambles and bushes, in many cases she was forced to waste valuable time hacking vines out of her path. Catching up to Delia would be impossible, but she persevered as best she could.

They were quickly out of sight, but less than a minute later she heard a roar that could only be an orcish battle cry. Islana struggled forward, heading toward the noise until she could see them again. She only spotted Mor Dai, however. Delia had vanished, and their vigilante companion was now surrounded by three heavily armed orc warriors.

Islana could see that one was limping, but between the three of them it was only a matter of time before they brought down the smaller man. Mor Dai was fighting valiantly to keep them at bay, but his rapier was a poor weapon against his heavily armored opponents.

Screaming her defiance to draw their attention, Islana advanced.

One of the orcs peeled away from the fight to meet her, leaving his two friends to harry Mor Dai. He carried a heavy wooden shield and a war hammer with an ugly metal spike on the end, an ideal weapon for facing an armored opponent.

For a second, Islana felt uncertain. She bore only her sword, her shield had been left with her horse, along with her mace. The longsword wasn't ideal for facing an opponent in mail, especially when he carried a shield. She would be at a disadvantage in size, strength, and weapon. Growling at her own fear she stepped forward.

The orc wasted no time. Grinning, he ignored her first slash and slammed his shield into Islana, knocking her off balance as he brought his hammer to bear.

She had expected the move. Dropping her sword, she grabbed the shield with both hands. It still struck her with tremendous force, but she kept her grip, falling back and pulling to twist her opponent out of position. The orc's hammer clipped the top of her helm, sending it spinning into the bushes, but doing her little harm.

Grappling with the orc, Islana managed to plant one foot behind his and shove, sending them both to the ground before he could strike at her again with the hammer. She landed on top of him, and while his greater strength still put her at a disadvantage, her weight hampered him even more. Islana levered herself over, temporarily pinning his weapon arm as she drew her misericorde.

The struggle was short and brutal, until at last she wedged the point of her long thin blade into the space between the top of the orc's breastplate and the crude leather of his gorget. One hard thrust and the orc was dying, the blade buried in his throat while he choked on his blood.

Disentangling herself Islana rose, bringing the dead orc's war hammer with her. She wanted the shield too, but it would have taken too long to retrieve. She waded into Mor Dai's fight with devastating results.

One orc turned toward her, but a feint from Mor Dai sent it's shield too high. Islana snapped the hammer out to shatter his knee and within seconds after that the fight was over.

Delia emerged from the brush then, carrying her bow and leading a young girl, "Looks like I missed the fun."

Mor Dai was panting, "Good triumphed nonetheless, thanks to our lady knight here." He dipped his head to Islana in a wordless gesture of gratitude. Blood was dripping from his scalp down one side of his face.

"That doesn't look good," said Islana. "Are you hurt anywhere else?"

A quick examination showed that the vigilante had suffered a scalp wound and a heavy bruise to one of his legs. Neither seemed serious, but his eyes had a strange look to them. Islana and Delia walked on either side of him as they made their way back to the road, in case he should fall.

They met the rest of their group as they emerged, and Sir Brevis scowled at Islana.

Her superior was not pleased.

CHAPTER 17
DARK STRANGER

Thomas watched while Sir Brevis spent long minutes giving Islana a thorough dressing down for her reckless action. He couldn't help but feel sympathy for her under the older man's withering barrage, but at the same time he was relieved. He wanted to yell at her himself.

Brevis finished with a curt, "Get that looked at," indicating a heavy bruise she had gotten during her recent fight. After that he turned away.

Thomas was standing close by, "Let me…"

"I can do it myself," Islana rebuked him, preparing to call upon her own hard won abilities to heal the injury.

He caught her hand in his own, "You might need your strength later—if there's another fight. You can heal yourself in combat. Let me use my power for now, so you can save your own for when it really counts…"

She met his eyes, and he could see something in them. She didn't speak, but after a second she nodded her assent.

Reaching inside himself, Thomas found the power Delwyn had granted him; his lips speaking soft words as her grace came forth. Running his fingers along her forearm he let the healing energies flow into her. When he was finished, he held onto her, "You scared me."

Islana frowned, "Despite what the Grandmaster said, I was acting according to my conscience. I wouldn't change that, even if I could."

Thomas nodded, "I know, but despite everything, I worry. I only hope She can forgive my selfishness."

She blinked, and when she replied her eyes held a challenge, "You could stand to be a little more selfish."

"What do you mean?" he asked.

Islana straightened, "The Goddess, the light, grows stronger when we share our joy." Turning away she took a few steps before adding, "Idiot."

Thomas heard her clearly, as she had meant for him to. Shaking his head, he looked around to see Grom and Delia watching from a few feet away. Glaring at them he challenged, "What?!"

They both shook their heads and Grom muttered, "Idiot indeed." The dwarf shook his head and moved off, but Delia stepped closer.

Leaning in, the ranger whispered in his ear, "Danger increases the appetite. Ordinarily I'd think to comfort you, but stupidity makes me angry. Especially when you continue to hurt my friend." She stalked after Grom without waiting for a reply.

The Abbott and the Grandmaster debated what to do about the child they had recovered and eventually they decided on a compromise. Rather than reduce their force by sending her back to the city with an escort, they chose Mor Dai for the task. He was mildly wounded already. Sending him back with the girl allowed them to conserve their healing and avoid diminishing their numbers.

The vigilante wasn't happy about the decision, but he saw the wisdom of it. Hoisting the girl in front of him, he left without much complaint.

The big question now, was where to go. The presence of orcs so close to the city was an indication of something serious.

"We should let our ranger search the area around their camp. There may be a larger encampment nearby," suggested Sir Brevis.

Father Whitmire was uncertain, "Or it might be a distraction..."

"It is a little of both," said the nobleman standing beside Thomas.

The Abbot glanced at him, his eyes widening, "Who are you?" Thomas and Sir Brevis did the same. No one had taken note of the stranger's arrival.

He wore a black doublet of fine cloth, something too soft to be velvet. It was matched by satin trousers and supple leather boots. The stranger's ears were adorned with silver earrings and he wore a silver chain around his neck to match. Everything about him spoke of understated wealth.

"Someone who would prefer to see you find your destination with a minimum of delays," answered the stranger.

Brevis snapped his fingers and several paladins moved to encircle the new arrival. "I think you had better explain yourself—quickly."

The newcomer glanced at Thomas from beneath black brows, his eyes as dark as his hair, "Thomas, surely you were expecting me, weren't you? Didn't you warn them?"

Thomas stared at him without recognition, but he remembered the dream, "Were you sent to...?"

The stranger smiled, showing teeth that seemed abnormally sharp, "... to guide you. Yes, that would be me."

"His dream," said Whitmire, grabbing Sir Brevis by the upper arm.

The paladin chuffed, "Even so, we should be certain we can trust him first." Placing one hand over his heart he let his eyes relax, unfocusing as he let his power surge forth.

The stranger's face took on a look of concern, "I don't think that would be wise..."

But it was too late. The senior paladin had opened his heart, an old technique that those of his order used to detect evil in others. Brevis' body stiffened, and then his eyes rolled back into his head. Seconds later he fell backward, his body beginning to twitch and thrash even as Whitmire caught his shoulders and eased him to the ground.

The Abbot looked up at the newcomer, worry and anger making the lines on his face much deeper, "You fiend. What are you?"

The paladins around him had drawn their blades, but the stranger took no notice of them. "I tried to warn him. You may call me Anthony, but I'm sure you'll understand that isn't my true name. I am here to guide you."

Thomas broke in, "You know where the Chalice is?"

Anthony nodded, but before he could speak Father Whitmire warned, "Thomas, we can't listen to this creature. Only a thing of immense evil could incapacitate Sir Brevis in such a way." The Abbot had the silver sunburst that represented his faith in hand as he faced the stranger, "You are not welcome here, whatever you may be."

Anthony laughed, "Foolish priest, would you turn away your goddess' most long-suffering ally?"

"You know where the Chalice is?" repeated Thomas.

"The Chalice is no longer of any consequence," said the stranger. Father Whitmire started to interrupt but Anthony held up a finger, and a shadow fell over the priest. The Abbot's mouth moved, but no sound emerged. "Try to speak over me again, mortal, and I may forget my promise to leave you unharmed."

The black garbed nobleman looked back at Thomas, "Now, where were we? Oh, yes, your search for the Chalice. You have more important things to worry about young man. What you seek now is not the Chalice, but your Lady, Delwyn herself.

"That Chalice has been used, its sacred purpose invoked, drawing the Morningflower into this world. Your enemies have her now, and they intend to use her. We must make haste before everything is undone."

"Impossible!" said Islana, outraged.

But Thomas already knew it was true. It matched perfectly with his dream. "How—no, what do they plan to do with her?"

Anthony stared back at him, "Those responsible seek power through anarchy, but their foolishness will only unleash a primordial darkness from its prison. To do so they must use a key, a key they have already stolen, but it is useless without the power to activate it, the power of your goddess."

Thomas' eyes went wide. The stranger could only mean one key, and the primordial darkness must then refer to... He stopped his thoughts there, *No, that can't be possible.* His mouth went on without him, "The Key of Anteri..."

Anthony glared at him, and Thomas' voice vanished. "Do not name me here!" he commanded. "The orcs you found here are deserters. Following their trail will only delay you. Your enemy used them to gain the stronghold of Baron Galway last week. They are using his keep for their ritual. Your goddess is there."

"Thomas, you can't trust him," declared Islana, her eyes worried as she saw him considering the newcomer's words. Sir Brevis groaned as if to underscore her point. The senior paladin was beginning to regain consciousness.

"I don't," said Thomas firmly, "but we need him. Our Lady told me he could guide us to her." At last he understood her message. He knew the stranger now, knew why he wanted to help them, and why he could never be trusted. Directing his gaze to Anthony, he made his decision, "Take me to her."

The shadow that had been over the Abbot had passed, and even though he had been unable to speak thus far, his ears had been working just fine. He understood the situation at least as well as Thomas, probably better. "Take *us* to her." Bending over he offered his hand to Brevis, helping his old friend regain his feet.

"That isn't necessary," responded Anthony. "I can take Thomas to her. The rest of you will only get in the way."

Thomas wanted to accept that. He didn't want to endanger his friends, most especially Islana, but his dream still echoed in his mind, *"...follow where he leads, but do not trust him."* Looking around, he caught Islana's eyes staring intently at him. There was strength there, and also a plea, she did not want to be left behind.

Leaving her—leaving *them* behind, would be foolish. His friends weren't children to be protected. His desire to shelter them was selfish and ultimately would only show a lack of respect. It might also make him a martyr. The mission had to come first, *Sarah* had to come first. Lifting his chin he addressed Anthony, "No. Where I go, they go. Delwyn did not invest her power in just one person, it is present here in all of us. We will undertake this together."

The stranger sighed, "If you ride to Galway's keep in force, the enemy will meet you with force, and he has much more of it at hand. There are at least fifty orc warriors guarding that place, as well as more 'unwholesome' allies."

Father Whitmire spoke up, "How were you planning to get in if Thomas went alone?"

"There is a small stream that runs around the castle. It keeps the moat filled and also provides fresh water to the inhabitants. At two points the castle wall is open to allow a portion of that stream to enter and exit the castle proper. Those places are guarded by heavy iron grates, but one, on the downstream side, near the postern gate, has rusted badly. There is a gap there that a man could pass through, provided the watchers on the wall don't spot him."

The Abbot glanced at Sir Brevis, hoping for his insight.

The paladin nodded, "I am against cooperating with this foul creature, but if you insist, four could pass almost as easily as one or two. The best way to draw the eyes of the defenders would be a serious threat. We can take our men down the road and approach openly. If they sally forth, we will face them. If they do not, we will seek entry. Whether we can gain access or not, the effort will draw their attention to the front gate, greatly improving your chances of entering unseen."

"Four?" asked the black garbed nobleman.

Sir Brevis nodded, "Thomas, Islana, Grom, and the ranger—five if you include yourself, hellspawn."

Anthony's eyes flashed in anger at the paladin's added insult, "I should rip that tongue of yours out to mend your tone, slave. If I do not go, Thomas will never reach her."

"Slave?" growled Brevis. "I serve for the glory of Delwyn. My conscience is clear."

The stranger stared back at the paladin, but after a moment his expression broke and he began to laugh, "Listen to the lapdog bark!"

Enraged, Sir Brevis started forward, hand already pulling his sword from its sheath, but Father Whitmire grabbed his shoulder. "Peace, Brevis! We cannot afford to fight him at this time!" ordered the Abbot.

Anthony smiled, "Swing that sword at me, paladin, and your goddess is lost. I might even leave you alive to despair at your failure, and to watch the world crumble into darkness with her absence."

"Why are you doing this?" asked Thomas suddenly. Anthony turned to him, ignoring the threat of the paladin, "You should know that already, little priest. I am bound by the covenant between myself and my cousin. Releasing the Beast would never be to my advantage. A better question, though, is why are *you* doing this? You are more tightly bound than any mortal or immortal that ever walked this earth. Do you never despair of your suffering? If there were anyone who might find peace in failure this day, it would be you."

"Don't listen to him, Thomas." It was Islana, standing close behind him now. "He's a liar. He's just trying to create doubt."

The look on Anthony's face was one of compassion as he answered her, "Love is the greatest source of tragedy in this world, far greater than me. You may find yourself cursing your goddess when you discover the price of her grace, lady paladin."

CHAPTER 18
BREAKING AND ENTERING

Sir Brevis rode at the head of the paladins, followed closely by the temple warriors. Father Whitmire and the other priests had donned armor, but they stayed at the rear of the formation. The castle of Baron Galway loomed before them, only fifty yards distant now.

The drawbridge was down and the gate had been smashed beyond any hope of usefulness. What remained of the portcullis had been wrenched and twisted from its customary place, it lay partly in the moat now, leaning against the drawbridge.

There were no watchmen visible on the walls.

"It appears our informant wasn't lying about the fall of the castle," observed the senior paladin as the Abbott rode forward to confer with him.

Whitmire nodded, "At least we don't have to worry about figuring out a way to get in. If the gate was operable they might have simply kept it closed and ignored us."

"I would still make sure they couldn't ignore us, but you are correct," answered the paladin. "We have a different problem now."

The Abbott waited for him to continue.

"If what that demon said is true, there could be as many as fifty orcs within. If they are manning the inside of the walls, we could enter only to find ourselves trapped and under fire from every side. If they're in the gatehouse we might find ourselves unable to escape back out the way we came in."

"If they're in the gatehouse, wouldn't they use the murder-holes to attack us as we first come in?" asked the priest.

Brevis shook his head, "Far better to let us get inside. They could finish us all without risk of any escaping to carry word back to the city. That's a large part of the purpose of the portcullis they destroyed, to prevent attackers that get inside from getting back out. At least that's gone. There's a possibility that even if we are ambushed, some of us might survive to ride back out."

"Our Lady is at risk," said the Abbot, "we cannot afford to fail. We won't get a second chance. We have to succeed, or die trying."

Glancing at the sun, Brevis nodded, "It's noon. They should be ready." Lifting his arm he motioned for them to advance.

The paladins' horses began to walk forward, while their riders raised their hands to their breastplates, placing them over the symbol of Delwyn as they prayed. The sunlight flared, and their armor began to shine as the goddess gave them her blessing.

Behind them the priests were praying as well, casting warding spells and protections over the warriors and blessing their weapons.

The horses were at a fast trot as they crossed the bridge and passed under the shadow cast by the gatehouse.

Everything remained quiet as they entered the courtyard, but as soon as the last horse had passed they heard a harsh voice bark a command.

Orcs stood up from their places along the walkways that topped the walls, broad grins on their faces as they lifted crossbows to their shoulders. The door to the inner keep was directly across from where they had entered, and it flew open to reveal a man in black robes while simultaneously a loud crack sounded behind them, and part of the gatehouse collapsed, blocking their exit with rubble.

They had expected the ambush, however. Standing in his stirrups Brevis yelled, "Left and right! Take the stairs, clear the wall!" Then he kicked his horse forward, charging toward the black robed man on the other side of the yard.

The paladins and temple warriors split into two groups, heading for the stairs inside the walls while Father Whitmire released the spell he had been holding at the ready. One final word left his lips as the orcs fired their crossbows, and a furious wind sprang up, whipping the air and sending the enemy quarrels veering off course.

Sir Brevis had almost closed with his quarry when the robed man opened his lips and uttered a word. The sound of it carried an unspeakable filth, and even the sunlight in the courtyard seemed to falter for a second. Most of the temple troops were too far away to hear it, but several of the closest fell instantly. Two of them were dead, and the third fell to the ground, paralyzed.

Brevis' faith protected him to a degree; the world went dark and silent as the unholy magic found his ears, but his horse was not so lucky. The loyal mount died under him, pitching him forward to tumble onto the rough ground. The paladin landed hard but managed to roll, preventing the worst of the damage from the fall. Scrambling to his feet, he realized he had lost his sword, but the worst of it was that he was blind.

Father Whitmire started to run forward, hoping to aid his friend, but a sound from behind alerted him to further trouble. Turning, he saw the source of the gatehouse's collapse. Stepping out from behind the rubble was a monstrous demon standing at least ten feet tall. Its skin was hard, almost shell-like, and one arm ended in a wicked looking claw.

Brevis would have to survive without him.

Drawing himself up, Whitmire lifted the golden emblem of his goddess, "You chose the wrong foe today, demon."

Thomas marched slowly through the dense forest. They were in a single file line; Delia led, and Islana followed her. Thomas was third in line and the stranger was behind him with Grom bringing up the rear.

They had been moving for over an hour, and to minimize noise there was no conversation. Consequently, Thomas had nothing to do but think—and watch Islana make her way through the brush ahead of him.

It wasn't a particularly idyllic view. The difficulties of moving through the heavy forest undergrowth spoiled Islana's usual athletic grace, and the armor did nothing for her figure, plus it stank. That was something the poets always ignored. In truth, of the four of them only Delia had a less than unpleasant odor, owing to the fact that she wore only hunting leathers. The armor worn by Islana, Thomas, and Grom, smelled of sweat and rust.

Thomas didn't include Anthony in his review of odors, since the man had no discernable scent whatsoever and was almost certainly not human anyway.

Thomas blocked the smells out and focused on other issues. Sarah was chief among them. He knew she was in trouble, and despite Islana's accusation he knew that Anthony had not lied. Indeed, the man was probably incapable of lying, if the teachings of the church were true. *Anteriolus, Prince of Hell and one of the principle evils, god of tyranny and suffering,* thought Thomas silently. *A creature of order and control, but also bound by cruel honesty. Of all the evils, only he is known to keep his word.*

He could almost feel the devil's eyes on his back as he thought the creature's name. A soft laugh confirmed his suspicion, Anteriolus could sense the use of his name, even when it was only within the confines of Thomas' thoughts.

The devil prince had also been the one to aid Delwyn in imprisoning Gravon the Beast. Theologians had argued about that point for ages, but it was generally agreed that he had done it because the Beast was a creature of chaos and entropy. Gravon had also been stronger than any of the other gods. Only by combining their efforts had they managed to trap him.

Sarah had said that he would guide him, and now that he knew who the stranger was, he understood why, but she had also warned him not to trust him. His mind kept returning to the Prince of Hell's words, *"You are more tightly bound than any mortal or immortal that ever walked this earth. Do you never despair of your suffering? If there were anyone who might find peace in failure this day, it would be you."*

What had he meant by that? Was he referring to the mark on Thomas' chest? Or perhaps it was the oath he had sworn to Sarah as a child? Was he doomed to become a martyr?

He found his eyes focused on Islana's back once more. *What would it be like to be married?* He wasn't sure if it was possible. If he was destined for some terrible fate, it wouldn't be fair to any woman who tied her happiness to his.

Islana stopped, and Thomas realized that Delia was holding up one hand. The ranger worked her way back to them and began whispering, "The edge of the stream is just ahead, and I could see the grate about twenty yards to our right. We have to be careful. The woods have been allowed to grow far too close to the wall, but we'll still have to step out into clear view for a short distance before we reach our goal."

They waited. There were two orcs in view along the top of the wall, and while they didn't look particularly vigilant, there was no way they could miss five people crossing from the edge of the forest to the wall.

Half an hour passed, and then they heard a commotion. Someone was yelling orders and the sound of arms clashing sounded clearly from the other side of the wall. Both of the orc watchers turned around.

"Now!" hissed Delia, and they broke cover and ran to the shadow at the base of the wall.

Once there, they were relatively safe. Even if the sentries turned their attention back, they were far less likely to spot them directly below in the darkened area where the stream emerged from the castle grate.

Unfortunately, the grate was far more substantial than they had expected. The bars that composed it were thicker than a big man's thumb, and while they did show signs of pitting and rusting, they appeared to still be intact.

"What now?" whispered Islana.

Their guide shrugged, but Grom stepped forward, "Let me take a look at it." The dwarf spent several minutes examining the metalwork and eventually waded into the stream searching the metal below the waterline with his hands. Eventually he grunted and gripped one of the bars. "Here. The foundation has washed loose and this one is no longer anchored."

"It's still too thick for us to bend it," observed Thomas.

"Nah, lad," said Grom. "This bar's badly pitted near the top, a weak point. It's a matter of leverage. If we pull from the farthest point, which happens to be the bottom, where it's no longer fixed..." Sitting down in the water the dwarf braced his feet against the bars on either side and wrapped his rough hands around the weakened one.

Grom's back shifted beneath his mail as he let out a low groan and began to pull. At first nothing happened, but after a moment the iron began to slowly bend. He managed to move it almost six inches from the base when the top abruptly snapped, and the brittle iron toppled to one side.

The gap provided was barely wide enough to fit them. Delia made it through without trouble, as did the stranger, but Thomas, Islana, and Grom were forced to remove their breastplates to slip through. The other side of the grate was a darkened archway beneath the wall which protected them from view. They took advantage of it to replace their armor before continuing.

"Where does it come out?" asked Thomas, wading up to Delia who had already moved forward to peer out.

"It looks like a separate courtyard," she answered. "The water cuts through the middle of it. There's a wall with an archway to the left and a door into something large built against the wall on the right, just beyond where the postern gate enters."

"The archway leads to the yard where the main gate is, the building you are looking at is the chapel," Anthony informed them. "That's where we will find her."

Thomas had managed to get a look for himself now, "It looks like it's dedicated to Delwyn. Why would they use one of her holy places?"

"Easier to invoke the chalice there," explained their guide, "and once it has been defiled it makes the perfect place for the ritual they are planning."

"If it weren't for the two on the wall, we could just walk to the church door," said Grom. "If we charge out of here we'll be sitting ducks for their crossbows. By the time we got up the stairs they'd have time to get off two or three shots each."

"Give me a minute," said Delia. Easing slowly out of the water to avoid splashing, she tucked her body in against the base of the wall just inside the courtyard. So long as neither guard happened to look directly at her, it wouldn't be easy to spot her. Reaching into a pouch at her waist, she drew out a tightly bound package of oilcloth. She revealed a bowstring as she unrolled it and within a minute she had strung her bow.

"Ye won't have time to get them both, girl," cautioned the dwarf.

"I only need a moment's distraction," said Delia.

Islana clapped Grom on the shoulder, "Make sure your helm is strapped tightly. You and I can run out. We'll take different directions. It will take them a while to react, and if we keep running, they'll have a difficult time making an accurate shot. By the time they get themselves together, Delia will have had all the time she needs."

"You're assumin' they aren't good shots," worried Grom.

"It isn't that easy to get a good shot on someone in armor, especially if they're moving," said Delia. "Even if they hit you it's likely to be a glancing shot."

Grom narrowed his eyes, "The same goes for you, lass."

She smiled confidently, "My targets will be standing still."

"Hang on a second," said Thomas. "We can stack the odds in our favor." Chanting for a moment, he put his hand on each of them to mark them with Delwyn's blessing, pausing only when he got to the last member of their band, Anthony.

The Prince of Hell lifted one brow wryly, "I'll pass, thanks."

With their preparations finished, Islana and Grom counted silently, mouthing the numbers at one another, when they reached 'ten', they clambered out of the stream in a rush and ran across the courtyard in separate directions. Their exit was noisy, and the water sloshing out of their boots made them slower than they expected.

As they ran Delia walked slowly and deliberately out from the wall, confident her companions frantic movements would hold her target's attention. Ten paces out she lifted her bow and drew it back until the fletching on her arrow was almost touching her ear.

The orcs had been startled by the sudden emergence of enemies beneath them, but since their crossbows were already loaded and cocked it didn't take them long to react. They had shouldered their weapons by the time Delia's first arrow flew.

Her aim was true, and the feathered shaft sprouted from the orc's right armpit before he could fire, with a grunt he fell back, dropping his weapon. A sharp crack announced the second sentry's shot, and a harsh dwarven yell accompanied by colorful swearing revealed that he had found his mark.

Delia nocked her second arrow and fired hastily, missing. The noise of her shaft breaking against the stone wall beside the orc alerted him to her presence, and he began hastily loading a fresh quarrel.

Time seemed to slow as she pulled yet another arrow from her quiver. Adrenaline was spoiling her usual dexterity, and only long practice kept the shaft between her fingers as she nocked it. From the corner of her eye Delia could see Islana charging back across the yard, heading for the stairs that led up to the top of the wall, but there was no way she could make it in time.

Taking a deep breath, she drew again, holding her bow at full extension for long seconds as she lined up her shot. The orc wasn't watching her, he was pulling on his crossbow, cocking it with brute strength. Delia exhaled slowly and relaxed her fingers. She knew she had hit her mark before the arrow left the string.

The shaft sprouted in the orc's right thigh, causing him to lose his hold on the crossbow and fall back against the stone merlon behind him. Islana reached him seconds later and finished him with a hard thrust of her sword.

Thomas was already by Grom's side, "Take it easy. I can fix this."

"Fuckin' orcs!" swore the dwarf, grimacing as he stared at the quarrel that had passed completely through his left calf. "Most hasty shots miss or glance off armor, she says—my ass!"

"I think she was right," said Thomas. "He just got lucky."

But Grom was having none of it, as Delia walked over he growled at her, "Why didn't you shoot that second one somewhere better? Like the throat or eye or somethin'!"

The ranger had recovered her calm by then, though she held her bow with both hands to hide the trembling of her fingers. "Hard to hit someone's throat when they're bent over a crossbow. His thigh was unarmored and it did the trick."

"That bastard deserved one in the dick for what he did to me!" spat Grom angrily.

Thomas broke the arrow in half and before Grom realized what he was doing he pulled the arrow through his friend's calf. Uttering a few quiet words, he laid one hand over the freely bleeding wound and let the goddess' power flow over it. His ability to channel Delwyn's power had grown greatly over the past year; within seconds the blood had stopped flowing and the skin had closed, leaving only a puckered red scar. "You should be able to walk on it," he told Grom.

Grom tested it carefully, surprised to find no pain when he stood. "Give the Lady my thanks, Thomas," he said at last, before adding, "Ahh me damn sock is full of blood. I'll be squelching in my boots."

Delia snickered at that but didn't bother mentioning that they were all already soaked from the waist down.

"Time is short," said their black clad guide. "The door to the sanctuary is over there."

The heavy oak doors that led into the castle chapel were barred from the inside.

"We'll have to find another way in," said Thomas.

"We don't have enough time," warned Anthony.

A heavy thunk announced Grom's solution. Jerking his axe free, he sent another heavy blow shuddering into the timbers. "That's for my leg!" he grumbled as he hacked at the wood.

CHAPTER 19
A DARK BARGAIN

Father Whitmire focused intently on his chant as the demon bore down on him. In the back of his mind an idle thought ran by, *I should have brought a shield.* Ignoring that thought, he finished his abjuration just before the demon's claw reached him, "In the name of Delwyn, I banish you back from whence you came!"

It froze, struggling against the cleric's authority and then began to fade.

Releasing a sigh of relief, the Abbot turned back to assist his friend.

Sir Brevis had lifted one hand to his eyes, calling on the goddess to lift the curse that had blinded him. When he removed it, he could see once more, but not soon enough to avoid the robed man's next spell. Green energy flickered around him, sapping his vitality.

The paladin staggered for a moment, but then he reached down and recovered his sword. Straightening up he marched toward the evil cleric, "I've had just about enough of you." Closing the distance he reached his foe before the other man could finish his next spell. Seconds later it was over.

Whitmire got there a moment later, "Are you alright?"

Brevis was panting, "I've felt better."

"Let me look at you," said the elder priest. "I think he siphoned away some of your lifeforce. If so, I'll need to repair the damage."

"It's not that bad," protested the paladin.

"It could do you permanent harm if I don't reverse the effect quickly," cautioned the Abbot.

"After we help the men clear the walls," said Brevis.

"We have definitely lost the element of surprise here," noted Delia as the dwarf's axe bit one more into the heavy wood. She held her bow up, an arrow nocked and ready.

Grom's efforts had removed a portion of the outer door and now the bar behind it was almost ready to give way. Islana stood close by, her sword ready.

Thomas was steadily chanting. After his prayer was finished he touched Grom's shoulder between swings and then moved on to touch the others, each in turn. Again, Anthony elected to forgo Delwyn's blessing.

"That should help protect both mind and body against the influence of evil," he told them. This next one will give your weapons the ability to pierce the defenses of those warded by dark magic. He started a new prayer, and when he was done he touched the arrow held ready on Delia's bow. He started to offer it to Islana but she shook her head.

The paladin was kneeling, her sword help up before her. The blade had already begun to glow with Delwyn's power.

Moving on, Thomas headed toward Grom, but it was then that the door gave way. The doors swung in as the heavy bar fell away, exposing a yawning darkness. There were no lights within and an ominous feeling emanated from the chapel. "I can't see a thing," complained Delia. "There's a spell of darkness over the interior," said Thomas. Lifting his hand to the sky he began to summon light. It would take more than a common spell to undo the magic inside, so he called upon the goddess to provide pure sunlight.

But Grom was already growling, "I can see it already." The dwarf was gripping the haft of his axe so hard that his knuckles had gone white.

Thomas finished his invocation, and a globe of pure golden light shot forward to burst within the interior of the chapel. It expanded rapidly, burning away the shadows and revealing a long aisle with pews on either side. The altar at the far end was smeared with something black, and grotesque symbols had been painted on the walls.

A hulking beast was in front of the altar. It stood over thirteen feet in height and great leathery wings were folded against its back. A massive iron sword was in its right hand and a heavy flail in its left, both were burning with angry red flames. The demons' crude lips drew back to reveal brown jagged fangs as it spoke, "Welcome to despair mortals."

Thomas' eyes went wide as his mouth went dry, and his heart knew fear. "It's a balor demon," he choked out. *It's over. There's no way to defeat something like that.*

Balor demons were the most powerful order of demons, their might only surpassed by that of their master, the Beast, Gravon. Only the strongest of divine entities, or the greatest of heroes, had a chance to oppose one.

What felt like an eternity passed as they stared at the dark guardian, and their fear only grew stronger as the moment stretched out. "Why isn't he moving?" whispered Delia at last.

"He is bound to the chapel, to prevent our passing," said Anthony matter-of-factly.

His words snapped Thomas' mind back into motion and he remembered who their guide was. Turning his head, he looked at the Prince of Hell, "Can you...?"

The diabolic god of evil smiled sadly, "No. My role in this matter is strictly circumscribed by certain rules. If I act on my own there will be greater consequences. Now, if I were to receive payment from a mortal, something great enough to match the task, I could provide my aid..."

"What sort of payment?" asked Thomas.

Anteriolus smiled, showing teeth that were entirely too sharp, "To remove something as great as a Balor demon? Even the soul of a devout servant of Delwyn's might not be enough, but yours might suffice."

Islana's jaw clenched, "Shut your mouth, defiler! Thomas would never agree to that." She never took her eyes off the balor, however, and cold sweat was dripping down her forehead and cheeks.

"I can see something behind him," announced Grom. "Like a black curtain or something."

"The entrance to the rear chamber. They are holding her there as they prepare the ritual," said Anteriolus.

"We don't have to defeat him, Thomas," said Islana. "We just need to occupy him long enough for you to get past and through that entrance."

"He'll slaughter you," protested Thomas. "I won't agree to that."

Islana straightened and turned to him, "I'm not giving you a choice." Her face was pale with fear, but then she reached out and grabbed him by the front of his mail shirt. Pulling him in she kissed him, hard. "That was for me...," she told him, "... but we are sworn to a greater purpose. *This* is for Our Lady, for Delwyn." Lifting her sword, she put her face toward the demon in the darkness. The blade began to glow even brighter as she marched purposefully into the defiled church.

As she moved into the chapel Islana began uttering the sacred oath of her order, "By the light of Delwyn, I bind your fate to mine, demon. I will smite you, and my sword will not rest until you are done, or I am dead trying!" A silver sunburst appeared on the monster's chest, and her armor and shield began glowing as if to match her sword. It was the first time she had ever called on Delwyn's wrath, and she knew it would probably also be the last, but she would not shirk her duty as a sacred defender of the goddess.

The balor smiled, "I will savor your heart's blood, little paladin, and wash it down with that of your goddess when this is done!"

A flash passed Islana as Delia's arrow flew toward the demon. She hit her mark, but despite Thomas' blessing the steel head merely bounced off the skin of the demon's neck. Grom roared his defiance and strode forward to join Islana in facing their foe.

The decision was already made. Thomas drew his sword and ran forward. Putting his hand on Islana's shoulder he cast the most powerful spell he had been granted that might aid her. It was one he had thought to use on himself if he were forced to fight alone, but given the circumstances it seemed better to put it on her.

Light pulsed from his hand and Islana's body grew, adding nearly a foot to her height and greatly increasing her strength. Her steps grew more confident, and she smiled briefly, "Thank you, Thomas."

By combining their powers and strengths Islana had become a weapon of the goddess and an opponent to be feared by any evildoer, but Thomas knew it was unlikely to be enough. The demon in front of them was on a completely different level. *But we have to try,* he thought. *Sarah is counting on us.*

Thomas was already beginning a new chant to bolster his companions as Grom and Islana came at the demon from either side. The creature merely laughed, ignoring them. The dwarf's axe bounced back without effect, but Islana's blade left a bleeding slash across his ribs.

The balor's eyes widened slightly, "That was a good cut, lady knight! Perhaps this will not be as boring as I thought. Let me reward you for your effort. My name is Dastrix." He lifted his left arm, swinging the burning flail in a wide arc, forcing them both to leap back and then he fixed his eyes on Delia who still stood just outside the doors of the chapel. "Since the ranger struck first I will grant her the first death."

Several more unintelligible phrases passed through his lips, and then Delia screamed. Looking back Thomas saw her skin ripple and twist as though it was trying to press itself into her body. Delia's bones stood out in stark relief and blood ran from her eyes and ears as she collapsed.

Islana and Grom attacked again, but the demon ignored them, lips moving over blackened teeth as he continued uttering phrases of unspeakable evil and pain. Delia's scream faded into a bubbling wheeze as he continued his magical assault.

"Break his concentration!" yelled Thomas as he went back to help his fallen friend.

Grom's axe struck the demon's unprotected neck but did little to distract him, but Islana had better luck. Lunging forward she thrust the point of her sword at Dastrix's bare stomach. It pierced the skin and sank inward several inches, smoke rising from the wound and black blood boiling out around the glowing metal. But the fiend never stopped chanting.

Raising one hand and making a complex gesture, Thomas invoked Delwyn's power again, this time using it to disrupt the fell energies swarming through Delia's body. For a moment he felt his will tested against the darkness, and his spirit quailed, but then he closed his eyes and thought of Sarah. A flash of red-gold hair crossed his mind, and he forgot his doubts, finishing the spell he felt the demon's grip on her dissipate. Delia fell silent. Her body was broken but her chest continued to move slightly, she was alive still.

Dastrix didn't hesitate. Once his spell was broken he brought his sword up and effortlessly deflected Islana's next strike. He ignored Grom entirely. Swinging his flail high and wide over the dwarf he used it to wrap past Islana's shield, sending the heavy iron balls crashing into the paladin's back.

Her armor held, but the bruising power of the blow sent her falling forward, close enough that she could smell the demon's fetid breath. From the side of her visor she saw Grom watching her. She raised her shield and caught a shivering blow from the sword on it as she pushed herself back, but her eyes were still on Grom.

The dwarf was too far back and to the side for the demon to see him clearly, making a gesture with one fist he dove forward. He rolled once and came up on his hands and knees behind Dastrix as Islana surged forward. She crouched low and drove in, using her shield to slam into the demon's chest.

Even with her increased mass and strength it might not have been enough, but Dastrix tried to step back and lost his footing when he encountered the dwarf behind him. Swaying, he toppled backward, crushing the wooden frame of the desecrated altar.

Islana followed him down, slipping her shield to the side and bracing the point of her sword against the balor's chest. When he hit the stone floor she put her weight into it, using that and her breastplate against the pommel to drive the blade home.

The demon's shriek of pain was deafening and Grom was trapped beneath its legs as he thrashed. She felt the sword pass through the monster's torso until it struck the hard stone of the chapel floor.

Releasing his flail, Dastrix clutched roughly at her backplate before flinging her across the small chapel like a ragdoll. With a deliberate kick, he sent Grom's battered body sliding down the aisle between the pews and then he rose slowly from the floor. "You will pay for this, bitch," hissed the demon, and then he used his free hand to pull the sword from his chest and fling it after the dwarf.

The longsword flew end over end, and the hard metal pommel struck hard against Grom's right eye as he struggled to rise. The dwarf's head rocked back, and he fell to the floor once more.

Dastrix's sword burned even hotter as he advanced across the chapel toward Islana. She had been stunned by the impact with the wall and was struggling to find her feet. Shattered wood and burning splinters flew as the demon destroyed the pews that blocked his path to her.

Islana looked up, her vision blurry as she watched her death approach. She was standing, but her sword was gone and her body felt sluggish as she tried to bring her shield up to block the rapidly descending sword. She wasn't going to make it.

Blinding light illuminated the chapel as a beam of distilled sunlight seared itself into her vision. The light pierced Dastrix and wrapped itself around his brutish form, becoming chains of golden fire. Smoke rose from the demon's coarse hair, and he screamed once more. Straining, the balor tried to shrug off the bonds of light, but despite his enormous strength they held.

As her vision cleared Islana saw Thomas standing in the doorway of the chapel. What seemed like liquid gold ran from his fingers, streaming across the empty space and connecting him to the chains that held the balor.

"Islana!" shouted Grom.

Shining metal turned over in the air as the dwarf threw her sword. Islana reached out and with almost inhuman grace she caught it neatly by the hilt. "Your time is done, demon," she told the fiend.

The balor's power was immense, and the chains were starting to stretch beyond their capacity, but there was fear in Dastrix's eyes as she prepared to strike again. Islana's sword was glowing ever brighter as she prepared to plunge the blade through his heart. She would not miss this time.

And then the sun shivered in the sky. The bright noontime sun flickered and dimmed as a shadow fell across the earth. The power in Islana's sword faded out, and the chains holding the demon dissolved into nothingness.

"No!" yelled Thomas, and Islana felt as though a hole had opened in her heart. The light had gone, leaving only emptiness. The power of their goddess had vanished. The support she had learned to rely on, the strength she had spent so much time training to use—was gone.

Dastrix drew himself up to his full height and laughed, "It has begun. You are too late."

Ignoring the soul shriveling fear that seemed to devour her heart, Islana thrust forward with her sword, but the tip skittered across the balor's now impenetrable hide. Sneering the demon swept across with his burning sword, and though she intercepted it with her shield the blade tore through the metal as though it were no more substantial than tissue.

The fell blade removed the top half of her shield and continued on, ripping through her pauldron and burying itself deep in her shoulder. Islana felt the black fire eating into her nerves as blood poured from her wound, and she sagged to the floor.

Dastrix pulled the sword free and then knelt over the now helpless paladin, using his claws to open the tear in Islana's breastplate. With very little effort the demon pulled the metal apart, exposing the dying woman's chest. "The heart tastes best when it is still beating," he whispered softly, licking rough lips with a tongue covered in festering sores.

CHAPTER 20
BLOOD PRICE

"I'll pay it," said Thomas, his voice desperate. "Whatever the cost, I'll pay it. Save her!"

Anteriolus stood beside him, "Swear it, in her name."

Without hesitation Thomas replied, "In Delwyn's name, I swear it. Save her, destroy this demon, and you may have my soul."

The Prince of Hell smiled and stepped into the darkened chapel, "Stop."

He said the word without emphasis, but Dastrix paused at the sound of his voice. "You have no business here, devil."

"I have taken a contract to end your life, fiend," said Anteriolus. "Your life is forfeit."

"My master is returning," answered the balor. "Interfere and he will crush you into dust."

"I created the prison he lies within," answered Anteriolus. "I doubt killing one more pathetic spawn of the Abyss will make much difference." Without seeming to hurry he had already closed the distance between them.

Dastrix swept his sword toward the Prince of Devils but Anteriolus caught it with seeming ease. His hand darted forward, fingers tipped by impossibly sharp claws.

It pierced the demon's chest and reappeared a second later, holding the balor's still beating heart.

The balor shuddered, his mouth open and fear written on his face.

"I'd eat it, but you aren't worth even that much," said Anteriolus. The balor's heart burst into flames and was quickly reduced to gray ash. It filtered between his fingers as the demon collapsed, dying in front of him.

Thomas was already kneeling over Islana's ruined body. There was blood everywhere, and the only sign that she still lived was the steady pulse as yet more pumped from the gaping wound in her shoulder. He reached for the magic Delwyn had given him, hoping he could save her life before it was too late, but the words wouldn't come.

He had felt it first when the sun had shivered. The Goddess wasn't there. His connection to Sarah had vanished. Something had happened to her; he was powerless.

Anteriolus reached past him, planting one finger in the bloody wound on her chest. Steam rose around it, accompanied by a sizzling sound, and then the flesh began to close. Islana's eyes flew open, and a gasp of pain passed her lips. She stared at the Prince of Hell, a look of shock and disgust on her features.

"Fear not, lady knight, my touch will not defile you—this time. The price has already been paid, and through no fault of your own," said Anteriolus.

Thomas looked away. He didn't regret his choice, but he couldn't bear for Islana to see the truth in his eyes.

"Save her, destroy the demon, those were your words, Thomas. I have fulfilled my end of the contract."

The devil smiled at him. "And I cannot help but feel it was indeed a *bargain,* for me."

Thomas straightened, resolving himself to whatever might come. "What happened? Is Sa—Delwyn dead?"

"No," answered Anteriolus. "She lives still, but the ritual has begun, sealing her power within her physical form. It will be minutes at most, before they bleed her dry to empower my key."

"How do I stop it?"

"The ritual binds her with chains that can only be broken by heartsblood. They intend for it to be hers...," the devil informed him. "...but any will serve. Enter the chamber and stab the priest of Gravon through the heart. His blood will dissolve her bonds and end the ritual."

Thomas stared at the strange shimmering black curtain, "Won't there be others with him?"

Anteriolus laughed, "Hah! The spawn of the Abyss are foolish and greedy. Whoever he is, he will not wish to share credit with any others. He will be alone, hoping to present himself as the Beast's sole deliverer."

Islana started to rise, her body was whole once more, but as soon as she lifted herself partway the blood drained from her face, and she collapsed. Thomas looked at the others, Grom was up now, moving slowly toward them, but it was obvious that he was in no shape for further combat. The dwarf could barely walk, and he had a noticeable limp. Delia was still unconscious at the entrance.

Thomas headed for the strange black curtain of energy that covered the archway behind the altar.

"Only those with singular intent can pass that barrier," warned Anteriolus. "If you were still connected to your goddess, you might manage it. Or I could destroy it...," suggested the devil.

"I have nothing left to pay," said Thomas. He stood in front of the barrier, staring at it as if his eyes could pierce it by force of will alone. "And nothing left to lose." He began to step forward.

"If your intent is not pure, whether for good or ill, the spell will rip the skin from your bones...," warned Anteriolus.

Thomas ignored him. In his mind's eye he saw only one thing now, Sarah's face. It was an image he remembered from his first day with her, when he had woken in her makeshift fruit-crate castle. Wild red hair and shining eyes, she had claimed him with that one look.

A cold chill passed over his skin as he stepped through the rippling darkness, and then he found himself standing in a small stone chamber.

A long flat-topped granite block dominated the center of the room. Sarah lay atop it, looking just as he remembered her, a child of perhaps twelve, with long wild hair and freckles. She was bound by something that looked like rope, but rather than being brown it was dark and hard in its appearance, as though it were some sort of flexible black iron.

The figure standing between them had wide, thick shoulders, covered by a black robe and hood. His back was turned, for he was facing his sacrifice, and Thomas saw his chance. Rushing forward, he drew his sword and made to stab the evil priest through the back, but the sound of his blade clearing its scabbard betrayed him.

The man spun, sending Thomas' point skittering along his back, tearing through the black robe and revealing iron mail beneath it. It also revealed his face, and Thomas saw that his opponent was no man at all, but rather an orc, greyish green skin stretched over a brutish skull, framing a mouth with two tusk-like canines.

The orc grinned, "Did you think I would be easy prey, human?" He held a dark iron dagger in his right hand, a weapon he had been about to plunge through Sarah's heart.

Thomas hesitated only a second before continuing his attack. The orc dodged his first slash and deflected the second with his dagger but the third he stopped by sweeping his mailed left arm across to knock the sword out of line. Rushing forward within reach, the orc punched forward with his shorter weapon, and Thomas only barely avoided being impaled by falling backward.

He was on the defensive, and he knew he had lost the initiative. The orc priest was stronger, faster, and at least as well armored. Even if his opponent had taken his first surprise attack, the sword probably wouldn't have pierced the heavy riveted mail that covered nearly the orc's entire body.

Backing in a circle around the stone altar, Thomas was forced to retreat to avoid a quick defeat. He was thinking furiously the entire time, though. Magic was no help, he had none while Sarah was bound and probably the only reason the orc hadn't bothered using his own power, was that he clearly had an overwhelming advantage over the smaller human already.

His sword was unlikely to get through the mail, so his only viable targets were the orc's hands and head, which were both unarmored. The feet were also a possibility, since they were only covered by heavy leather boots. Unfortunately, the evil cleric was just as aware of those things and gave him little opportunity to reach those targets.

The length of his blade gave him one advantage, though, reach. He probed constantly as he fell back before the orc's advance. A lunge at the orc's foot would force him to step back, but higher attacks he merely batted aside with his forearms, and each time he came closer to gutting Thomas.

My mail would probably save me, but if he gets close enough to get his hands on me it will become a grapple, and there's only one way that will end, Thomas thought.

Desperate, he took a chance, swinging wide and high he took aim at the cleric's head, but when the arm came up to guard it he had already shifted his strike to come up short. Flicking his blade up into a short backstroke, he clipped the orc's hand, nearly severing the thumb.

His small triumph was short-lived, however, for his foe ignored the injury and took advantage of the pause in Thomas' retreat. Stepping forward more rapidly than before, the evil cleric drove his dagger into the human's stomach.

Thomas saw his mistake in the last second. His opponent hadn't forgone magic, he had merely performed it so quietly and quickly that Thomas hadn't noticed it. The dagger had a spell on it, one that wasn't considered very powerful, for it was only good for one attack, but it made certain that that one attack would almost certainly find its mark.

The wind was driven from his lungs as the iron blade drove the chainmail and padding over his sternum inward, and then pain, as the mail parted and cold metal entered his belly. He gaped at the orc as he staggered back, covering his midsection with his left hand.

The orc raised his left hand to display his wounded hand, "A fair trade!"

Thomas couldn't breathe. Glancing down he saw that his hand was covered in blood. There was surprisingly little pain, but he was surely dying. Sidestepping, he reached out with his left hand and smeared some of the blood over Sarah's bonds. Nothing happened.

His enemy laughed, "Heart's blood little man, only heart's blood! I aimed too low for that trick to work." Rushing forward the orc punched Thomas in the chest, sending him flying back against the wall.

Sliding down the wall, Thomas watched in horror as the cleric lifted his iron blade over the goddess once more, growling, "Let's finish this while you're still alive to watch, little man."

Despite the passage of years and the vast differences, in that moment it seemed much the same as the day his childhood nemesis, Flin, had attempted to crush the kitten beneath his foot, and Thomas' response was nearly identical. Leaping forward with strength he hadn't known he possessed, Thomas threw himself across Sarah's chest.

His body spasmed with white-hot pain as the cold iron plunged through the space between his shoulders, ripping through nerves, muscles, and heart before the point emerged on the other side. The world grew dark as he stared into Sarah's eyes, their faces only inches apart as he died. *I'm sorry, this was the best I could...*

Scarlet blood ran freely from his ruined body as his head sagged to lay quietly against Delwyn's neck. And then the black bonds that held her began to dissolve...

Father Whitmire felt the change even as the sun flared in the sky. It was as though a veil had been drawn back, exposing his soul, nay, his entire being to the burning light that hung above them in the heavens. Delwyn was free, but her heart was full of rage. Her wrath poured down, and the sunlight felt like golden fire scouring the wickedness from the world.

The Abbot and remaining soldiers and paladins went to their knees. Only Father Whitmire raised his face to the burning sun, exclaiming, "Goddess please, have mercy upon us!"

As if in answer, the castle began to shake and a pillar of fire shot up from somewhere in the adjoining courtyard. The blazing flames stretched up and up, ever higher until it seemed they would reach the sun itself.

Whitmire was blinded by the light, and the voice that shook the world threatened to burst his eardrums, "Give him back!"

Chapter 21
Endings and Beginnings

Thomas was floating, but he knew not where. He was surrounded by an endless white fog. At first that didn't bother him, until he began trying to look around. It was the same in every direction, so much so that he wasn't certain if he was turning his head or if he was stationary. Then he realized he couldn't find his hands, or any other part of his body. For all he could tell there was nothing to him, just an aimless viewpoint on an endless and never varying vista.

"You have crossed a line, taking what does not belong to you." It was Sarah's voice and it was a relief, the sound of it gave Thomas something to focus on. He was not alone. He tried to answer, but his own voice was just as absent as the rest of his body.

"He made the bargain of his own free will," answered the voice of Anteriolus. "It was good that he did, or you might have died this time and everything we have wrought would be undone."

"He is *mine*! You have no right. He does not belong in…"

"*Yours?*" interrupted Anteriolus. "Not any longer, he has made his choice."

"This goes against our agreement," argued the goddess.

"No, he changed it. Why don't you stop being so self-righteous for a change? Do you really think I would take him to Hell? I'm doing him a favor. I will see him reborn, but in the next life he won't be forced to suffer your tender torment. He will have power, and every delight the mortal world can offer to those who rule in my name! It's long past time he is freed from your pointless cycle of never-ending martyrdom."

"That cycle is all that protects the precious world you are constantly seeking to dominate! It was his choice to accept the burden..." began the sun goddess.

"And it was his choice to change his allegiance!" finished Anteriolus. "My son deserves better!"

"He is my son too!" she said bitterly. "I won't let you do this."

"You have no choice this time," replied the Prince of Hell.

Delwyn's voice changed its tone then, becoming sly, "Perhaps you have forgotten something?"

"How did you get that?" asked the devil. "That doesn't belong to you."

"The servant of the Beast left it lying on the ground when I slew him," said Delwyn.

"You aren't allowed to claim things in the mortal realm, not without a bargain."

"I didn't travel there of my own will," replied the goddess. "I was summoned in my own body. I was free to do as I wished once the ritual was broken. Now your *key* is mine."

Anteriolus laughed, "Now who is threatening the end of the world? You would risk everything to get him back?"

"I would."

"You're insane."

The goddess responded immediately, "You're one to talk."

"Very well, I will agree to an exchange, on one condition," offered Anteriolus.

"Which is?"

"Revive him. Let him finish this life before sending him on to the next. He deserves a respite from your games," said the Prince of Hell.

"You surprise me," replied the goddess. "I thought you sacrificed all of your compassion and mercy when you created the prison. Did you hold something back?"

"I still have pride in my offspring," said the devil.

"And you're one to talk. Your jealousy over him practically reeks of selfishness. Perhaps you did not give as much as you said either?"

"Thomas."

He opened his eyes at the voice, and found Sarah staring down at him with a serious expression. "I thought I heard you talking," he told her.

"I wondered if you heard," she replied, glancing away momentarily. "The memory will fade soon." The ceiling of the chapel was gone and the sun was eclipsed by her face, it filtered through her hair and wrapped him in a blanket of rose-gold light.

"If you're my…," he paused for a second, "…my mother, how—why him? Isn't he your enemy?"

"The gods are not as simple as theology describes, nor are we unchanging. Anteriolus was not always evil, and I was not always good. To create the prison, the key, and *you*, we each sacrificed parts of ourselves, becoming as you see us now. I gave my selfishness and greed, while he gave his compassion and mercy, but even now we are not entirely devoid of the things we originally divested ourselves of, you have seen and heard that for yourself."

Thomas processed that for a while before asking, "Then what am I?"

She smiled, "Just a man, in this life at least; you have been both men and women in your past lives. You are what is left of the being we created to challenge the beast and bind him in our prison."

"Why did he make a key?" said Thomas. "It seems like a foolish thing to do."

She shook her head, "Every cage has a door. A key had to be made. Eventually we will fail, and the Beast will be released again. The prison will be destroyed, and *you* will be restored to what you were when we first made you, but the world would not survive the war that would follow, and it is possible we would lose next time."

"The chalice is another part of it," added Delwyn. "It is necessary to empower the key, as you have seen. It will have to be remade, that will be a task for your remaining days."

He thought about it for a moment, "What if I don't? I can understand why it and the key were initially created, but if it is gone now, it would be safer to leave things as they are. Then the Beast could never be freed."

"Without the chalice, the prison will crumble, slowly but surely. Perhaps not in this lifetime, but within a few generations, the Beast would be free. Creating it anew will restore the binding that keeps it locked away," explained the goddess.

"How will I make such a thing?"

"That you will have to learn for yourself, but it will take everything you have, everything you are. The final step will require you to surrender your life."

Thomas sighed, looking at the devastation around him. The chapel had been blasted and scoured clean by whatever Delwyn had done when she had been released. It seemed a perfect match for the dark news she had just delivered. "So, I have to die after all..." For some reason that thought conjured an image in his mind, Islana. Nothing was ever fair.

The goddess leaned forward and kissed his forehead, "Someday, but it can wait for as long as you wish. Live, Thomas, grow old. The final step doesn't have to be taken until you are ready for it."

He felt her power taking hold, and his eyes grew heavy, sleep would soon overtake him, but he fought against it. "Sleep, Thomas, things will be better when you awaken," she told him.

"But, you said I would forget. How will I know what to do?"

"The answers will find you, with time, and your heart will always remember—when your mind rests and sleep brings us together again."

He awoke in a dimly lit room. Light filtered in from a high window, and he found himself wrapped in warm blankets. Thomas wasn't sure where he was, but the style of the woodwork made him think he might be back in the temple in Port Weston.

Thomas closed his eyes again. He hadn't wanted to wake up. He had been having a beautiful dream, the sort that left him wistful and sad as it faded from his waking mind. *I found my mother, I wasn't an orphan anymore.* He could almost see her, feel her presence, but the misty happiness of his dream was rapidly vanishing, leaving behind an aching loneliness.

Please, don't go, but it was too late. It had just been a dream, and he was still just an orphan, a man without roots or family. Thomas sat up in the bed and felt hot tears spill down his cheeks.

The door clicked as it opened, and he wiped his face rapidly with the blankets, embarrassed that someone might find him crying over something as silly as a dream.

"Thomas?" Islana stood in the doorway clad in a simple woolen robe. That was enough to confirm his suspicion; she would never be wearing something so casual if they weren't at home.

Home, he thought, *I suppose that's what this is.* He had never really considered it before. "How is your shoulder?" he asked, hoping she hadn't noticed him rubbing his eyes a moment before.

She frowned, "It's fine. There isn't even a scar. If I didn't have such a vivid memory of receiving the wound I would think I had imagined it. That's not what bothers me the most, though."

He smiled, "What could bother you more than that?"

"The man that healed me, and how he was paid for it."

"Oh," he said simply, not sure how to answer. His memories of the time afterward were already gone, but there were a few things he knew. "You don't have to worry; I'm not a servant of Hell. She bargained to get me back."

"Father Whitmire told us," said Islana.

Thomas raised his brows in surprise.

"She spoke with him afterward. That wasn't what bothered me."

"What then?"

"You sold your soul for me, Thomas. You didn't know you would get it back. No one should do something like that," she explained. After a second she asked, "Was he really...?"

"The Prince of Hell?"

"Yes."

Thomas nodded, "I don't remember everything well, but I don't think he was as terrible as you might think. I got the impression he and Delwyn were old friends."

"That's not the point, anyway," she replied. "You didn't know she would save you. I'm not worth that, no one is."

He laughed, "A simple 'thank you' would suffice."

She glared at him, "I'm not thanking you! You nearly damned yourself! How do you think I would have felt if you hadn't come back?"

Thomas stared up at the window. She was right, of course. "I didn't do it for you," he lied. "I did it for Our

Lady. You shouldn't blame yourself." It wasn't the truth, but it wasn't a complete lie.

The bed moved, and he looked back to see that she had sat down on the edge of the bed. For a moment, he was acutely aware of the fact that he wasn't wearing any clothes. He pulled the blankets a little farther up self-consciously.

Islana decided to change the subject, "When they found you there was blood everywhere, and there was a tear in your mail, front and back. What happened?"

He *did* remember that part very clearly, and for a second he felt again the searing pain as the blade tore through him. "The bonds holding her, holding the goddess, they could only be broken by heart's blood, just as Anteriolus told us. I fought with an orc, but I wasn't good enough to beat him. Getting between his blade and the Lady was the only way I could stop him."

"Getting stabbed through the heart is the absolute dumbest way to save someone," she chided, a wry smile on her face. "Next time you should introduce me to your orc friends instead."

Thomas chuckled for a moment before stopping to study her face. He could tell she had been worrying for days, but despite the circles under her eyes he found himself captivated once more. Without thought he leaned toward her—until she lifted her hand to gently push him back.

Embarrassed, he felt his face flushing, "I'm sorry, I thought..."

"Don't toy with me, Thomas. I couldn't take that."

"Well, before, when we were facing the balor...," he began.

Islana shook her head, "That was *me*. I already know I'm serious, besides I was feeling selfish. And we're not about to fight some horrible demon right now."

At last he understood. Catching her arm before she could rise and distance herself, he answered, "I've never been anything *but* serious about you, Islana. At one point I was too serious, about you, and my duty, but that isn't the case anymore."

She stared back at him, challenging him with her eyes, "What's changed?"

"I think we've earned the right to our own happiness," he told her honestly. "In fact, while I don't remember it, I *think* they might have told me that directly."

"Finally," she sighed, and then she leaned in, closing her eyes.

The moment stretched out over the space of several dozen heartbeats before Thomas reluctantly pulled his lips away from hers. "Will you marry me?"

The words startled Islana, and she jerked back. One leg was caught on the bed and the other in no position to support her sudden motion, and she wound up toppling unceremoniously to the floor at the bedside. "What the hell, Thomas!? You can't just leap out at someone with a question like that!" Flustered, she gathered her legs under her and stood, taking a few steps away to gain some perspective.

Unwilling to let another mistake derail their relationship, Thomas leapt up from the bed, catching her hands between his own, "Don't run away. Maybe it's too soon to ask that—you're right. What about another picnic?" He added the last while giving her what he hoped was his most charming smile.

Islana went stiff as he latched onto her hands, her face turning slowly red, and her eyes darting briefly downward.

Thomas began to blush as well when a draft of air reminded him that he still wasn't wearing anything, but he refused to let go until she had answered him. Clenching his jaw, he gave her a determined look.

"If I say yes, will you put some clothes on?"

He nodded.

"Yes then." She had recovered from her shock and was beginning to grin at his embarrassment.

Thomas let go of her hands and began to cast about for something to cover himself with. He started to pull one of the coverlets from the bed when he spotted a linen shift draped over the footboard. Reaching for it he glanced back at her, "You could cover your eyes, or turn around at least."

"Who am I to turn away from the vision that the gods have so freely offered me?" she laughed boldly.

Once he had the shift on she walked to the door, "I'll wait outside while you finish dressing."

Thomas smirked, "What's the point? You've already spoiled my good reputation. Now I'll never be able to get married."

"Maybe I'll take pity on you," laughed Islana as she opened the door, but her laugh stopped cold when she discovered Delia standing just outside with one hand to her ear. Grom leaned against the wall on the other side of the hallway.

There was a twinkle in the ranger's eyes as she looked up slightly at the taller woman, "I have to hand it to you, you don't waste any time." She glanced past the paladin to where she could see Thomas struggling to pull his hose on.

Grom chimed in, "I'm pretty sure it was innocent. I din't hear any yowlin'."

Islana put a hand over her face. It was still early, and she could already see how the rest of her day was going to turn out.

Coming in 2017

DEMONHOME

Matthew Illeniel seeks the source of the intruders into his world, traveling across dimensions to find answers. He must unravel the mystery of the She'Har's great enemy but the bigger challenge may lie in discovering the secrets of humanity itself.

For more information about the Mageborn series check out the author's Facebook page:

https://www.facebook.com/MagebornAuthor

or visit the website:

http://www.magebornbooks.com/

Printed in Great Britain
by Amazon